D1032372

Growing up

DAVID ROSSOF

A BAR MITZVA

Growing up

TORY

ELDHEIM PUBLISHERS
Jerusalem / New York

edited by Shimon Hurwitz

illustrated by I. A. Kaufman

שנת ב"ן י"ג א"ל עו"ל מצוו"ת (תשד"מ) לפ"ק

First published 1984
ISBN 0-87306-370-8

Copyright © 1984 by
David Rossoff

All rights reserved

No part of this publication may be translated,
reproduced, stored in a retrieval system or transmitted,
in any form or by any means,
electronic, mechanical, photocopying, recording or otherwise,
without prior permission in writing from the author.

Distributed by

Philipp Feldheim Inc.
200 Airport Executive Park
Spring Valley, NY 10977

96 East Broadway
New York, NY 10002

Feldheim Publishers Ltd
POB 6525 / Jerusalem, Israel

Printed in Israel

Contents

ב״ה

RAV SIMON SCHWAB
736 WEST 186TH STREET
NEW YORK, N. Y. 10033

RES: 927-0498
OFFICE: 923-5936

שמעון שוואב
אב״ד דק״ק
קהל עדת ישרון
נוא־יארק, נ.י.

ערב חנוכה תשמ״ג

This book, **GROWING UP**, will make many a בר מצוה boy very happy, especially if he begins to read it half a year prior to his 13th birthday. He will learn a great deal about הלכות pertaining to תפילין and he will – at the same time – absorb a plentiful portion of מוסר and יראת שמים, told by the author whose skill makes learning a pleasure.

I don't think any הסכמה is necessary, certainly not one from me.

בברכת הצלחה!

שמעון שוואב

ב״ה

בית דין צדק

לכל מקהלות האשכנזים
ע״י העדה החרדית פרו״ח
בעיה״ק ירושלם תובב״א
ת. ד. 5006

BETH DIN ZEDEK

of the Orthodox
Jewish community

JERUSALEM P.O.B. 5006

Tel. 222808 טלפון

פעיה״ק ירושלם ת״ו יום כ״ח לחדש שבט שנת תשמ״ד №............

יקר סהדותא

הננו בזה להגיד בשבחו של האי גברא יקירא הרה״ח ה״ר דוד רוסוף שליט״א, שעוסק בזיכוי הרבים לקרב ישראל לאביהם שבשמים, במה שמתרגם עניני תורה ויר״ש להבינם לנחוצים לכך.

הננו לברכו שיהא לו סייעתא דשמיא להגדיל תורה ולהאדירה בפעליו הברוכות.

וח״פ בהוראת הגאוה״צ הביד״צ שליט״א

Preface

This book is an English adaptation of the popular Hebrew *sefer*, "The Time of Young Manhood and Bar Mitzvah" (Part I),* by Rabbi Daniel Frish of Jerusalem. Rabbi Frish collected a wide selection of traditional sources, successfully weaving together stories, *halacha* and *mussar* for the young reader entering Jewish manhood. At this age, perceptive guidance and thoughtful encouragement are very much needed. These purposes have also prompted this English adaptation in order to reach out to even more young people.

With the author's consent, many textual additions and editorial changes have been made in order to make the book more suitable for the English-reading audience. Moreover, an entire tefillin handbook has been written to help the novice in this all-important mitzvah. Our hope is that the final product has cast Rabbi Frish's work into a contemporary mold, easy-to-read and refreshingly informative.

This effort was not a simple transformation, and I thank *HaKadosh Baruch Hu* for His *chesed* in facilitating the process. Further, I would like to thank the many who gave freely of their time and scholarly advice. Among them were Rabbi Yaakov Hillel, Rosh Yeshiva of Ahavath Shalom; Rabbi Aharon Feldman, Rosh Yeshiva of Ohr Sameach; Rabbi Israel M. Zacharish; Rabbi A. Abraham; Rabbi David Oppen, Director of

*The title in Hebrew is ימי הבחרות: הבר מצוה, Jerusalem, 1981, 5th edition.

Machon Devora; Rabbi Yaakov Levi; Rabbi Aryeh Carmell and Mr. and Mrs. Yechezkel Goldfield. Their comments, suggestions and criticisms were invaluable. Gratitude is also expressed to my father-in-law, Mr. Sherman Shapiro, for his kind encouragement.

The editor, my dear friend Shimon Hurwitz, worked diligently to develop every passage's readability. Without his technical advice, the book could not have reached its present form.

The *perush* to the Thirteen Principles was based on the Rambam's own commentary and on Rabbi S.A. Agassi's remarkable booklet, *Foundations of the Torah*.

Concerning the illustrations, no attempt has been made to depict the actual faces of the different *rebbes* and *chachamim*; rather, they are merely aids in stimulating the reader's imagination.

Throughout this entire project my wife, Devora Faige תחי׳, was "like a fruitful vine in the recesses of the house," creating an atmosphere in which I was free to complete this work. Our *tefillah* is that our sons, Yaakov Lipa, Bezalel, Eliyahu Meir and Yosef Leib, נ״י will enter their Bar Mitzvah with a deep sense of Torah values and with their hearts full of inspiration for the tasks that await them in life.

This volume is dedicated to all the young men who are beginning in the ways of full Torah service. May the guidance which they find in these pages help lead them along the pathways of Torah and bring the footsteps of the *Moshiach* closer and closer.

Introduction

As a young boy approaches his Bar Mitzvah, a new world opens before him: the world of manhood. The Torah, as explained by *Chazal*,* declares that at thirteen a boy reaches Jewish manhood and is obligated like every adult to fulfill all the commandments of the Torah.

This change in the life of a young Jew can appear to be external. Now he will start wearing tefillin, be counted in a minyan, and be allowed to read the *Sefer Torah* publicly in shul. He will get a new suit and lots of presents and have a special party. That much he knows. But the deeper meaning of Bar Mitzvah is often unclear and remote to him since the externals often cloud the real picture inside.

Jewish manhood, however, is not just a measure of years. Rather, it shows a qualitative growth in character. When Dovid *HaMelech* was on his deathbed, he instructed his son Shlomo, "Be strong and be a man." The *Targum* on this verse explains, "Be strong and be a man *who fears sin*," for Jewish manhood means a growing awareness of one's responsibility to act righteously both towards HaShem and towards one's fellow man.

This increased understanding has many practical consequences for the young Jewish person. He senses a more serious attitude towards his Torah

* See glossary for explanation of Hebrew terms.

study and fulfillment of mitzvoth. He responds more maturely and respectfully in his relationships with parents, family, teachers and friends. His sense of community responsibility and group involvement is heightened. His heart becomes more open to prayer and character improvement *(mussar)*.

All these positive developments are a factor of greater mental and physical growth. Precisely at this point comes the obligation to fulfill Torah and mitzvoth, for they enable the individual to begin controlling his selfishness and physical desires. For example, tefillin show us that the mind is to be trained in order to control the body. The knot of the *shel rosh* is placed where the brain connects with the spinal column and the straps continue downward to the lower parts of the body, both these facts indicating that we must apply Torah thoughts and rules for the proper use of the body.

The building of a more perfect character is one of the basic purposes of Torah Judaism. The process is guided and developed not only through learning Torah and doing mitzvoth, but also through following our historic Jewish models: the *Avoth,* the heroes in *Tenach*, the *Tannaim* and *Amoroim*, the *Rishonim* and *Acharonim*, the famous Torah *rebbeim* and Chassidic *rebbes*, the leaders of our own generation. With all these aids to greater self-improvement, the Bar Mitzvah young man should be aware that he is beginning on the serious road of Jewish manhood. This road is a step-by-step process — not automatic or instantaneous — but at least *now* he has started, and *now* he is personally responsible for the success of the journey.

The goal of this book, with HaShem's help, is to aid the Bar Mitzvah young man see clearly the importance and specialness of his new position in life. Further, we have endeavored to provide the basic information which he needs in order to make of his Bar Mitzvah a successful first step in the direction of full Jewish manhood. Finally, with the "Tefillin Handbook" we have enabled every Jew to learn and review the laws of tefillin in a concise, but complete fashion.

1 / *The big number*

Jerry and Sammy Goldstein were walking briskly to shul in order to make the *Maariv** service. They were both excited about tomorrow morning's trip to New York to attend cousin Joshua's Bar Mitzvah.

"I'm telling you, Sammy, the Bar Mitzvah is about the biggest thing you can imagine," Jerry was telling his younger brother. "I'll always remember the speech which I gave. Do you remember?"

"A little bit," answered Sammy. "That was almost three years ago, you know."

"You were running around so much then, but now you'll see for yourself at cousin Josh's Bar Mitzvah. Remember, your Bar Mitzvah isn't so long away any more."

"Six months."

"So you'd better start getting ready now."

* See glossary for explanation of Hebrew terms.

"I have. Rabbi Adler gives me lessons once a week."

"I know, but that's for learning the *leining* and the *haftorah*. What I mean is something else."

"What do you mean?" Sammy looked at him in surprise.

"I mean that everything is different. Now it's all for real."

"What? I do all the mitzvoth just like you," Sammy was reacting personally to Jerry's comment. "In fact, I ate my matzah at the *Seder* faster than you did. And next week on *Shavuoth*, I'll be learning all night right with you. I learn *Chumash* and *Mishna* and *Gemora*. I pray three times a day, I..."

"Okay. Don't get so upset," Jerry smiled."But tell me: do you *daven* with tefillin on?"

"No," admitted Sammy, "but that's about the only thing. Besides, I do the mitzvoth the same as you — *Kiddush* on Shabbat and Yom Tov, listening to Mom and Dad when they tell me to do things, and studying Torah. And I'm always careful to say *b'li neder* before I promise to do anything. So, don't you see, tefillin is really about the only thing.

"So what's the big thing?" protested Sammy. "Tefillin and the big *simcha*; *great*. I'm already a hundred percent Jewish. How do I add anything more when I become Bar Mitzvah?"

They were waiting for the light to change at the corner of Glen Avenue.

"Well," Jerry seemed to be thinking out loud. "Well, first of all, everything is more serious. For example, now it really matters — in the eyes of the Torah — that I eat the matzah on the *Seder* night. I'm under direct command and I have to eat it."

"And you have to drink wine on *Purim*, too."

"That's right. Now it's not so much what *I* want to do, it's what *HaShem* tells me to do. Fast one day, drink the next, recite the *Haggadah*, shake the *arba-minim*, learn Torah, *daven* — yes, it's serious business doing the *Taryag mitzvoth* properly. But then growing up is what HaShem wants from us."

"The light is green," interrupted Sammy.

After they crossed the street, Jerry glanced at his watch.

"Wow, Sammy. Only a minute 'til *Maariv*, let's go. We'll talk more about this on the way home."

After they finished *Maariv* and counted the *Omer* and were on their way home, Jerry continued the conversation from a different approach.

"Sammy, thirteen is a really big number, isn't it?"

"Yeh?" asked Sammy.

"In fact," continued Jerry, "in some ways, it is even bigger than fourteen, fifteen, or any other number. It has a special importance that makes it really stand out. For example, thirteen stands for oneness."

Sammy looked at his brother in surprise. "How does thirteen equal oneness?"

"Take the Hebrew word for one, *echod* [אֶחָד] and add up the value of its letters like this: *Alef* [א] is one, *chet* [ח] is eight, *dalet* [ד] is four — one, eight and four add up to thirteen. *Echod* is thirteen and thirteen is one."

"Oh, now I understand."

"Thirteen also represents love," continued Jerry. "The *gematria* of *ahavah* [אַהֲבָה], which means love, is thirteen: *alef*

[א] is one, each *hei* [ה] is five, and the *beit* [ב] is two — a total of thirteen. Something, yeh?"

"Boy, it sure is."

As the pair approached another intersection, Jerry looked up at the streetlight and thought for a moment. "You know, the *Chumash* also discusses the importance of the number thirteen. In *Bereishith*, when HaShem promised Avraham, 'And I will make your name great,' Rashi says that this is why we say 'the G-d of Yaakov' in the *Shemone Esre*. In Rabbi Elias Schwartz's book *V'shee-non-tom*, he brings a saying of *Chazal* which explains why we say 'G-d of Yaakov' and not 'G-d of Yisroel.' Did you ever hear about this?"

"No, I don't think so."

"Simply, the names of our three forefathers Avraham, Yitzchak and Yaakov have a total of thirteen Hebrew letters. If the name Yisroel were used instead of Yaakov, the total number of letters of the *Avoth* would be more than thirteen. And thirteen, as I just told you, is a very important number. It stands for *echod*, the One, the Oneness of HaShem. Therefore, when we reach Bar Mitzvah, we are able to bring His Oneness into the world. And you want to know why, Sammy? Because as soon as we do the mitzvoth, we show to the whole world that HaShem is the One in charge of everything.

"Also, our great grand-mothers, Sarah, Rivkah, Rochel and Leah, are a symbol of the Oneness of HaShem in the same way. The total number of letters in their Hebrew names adds up to thirteen, *echod*, and together they spread their motherly love, *ahavah*, to all of their children for all generations.

"Now listen to this, Sammy," Jerry said excitedly. He was talented in mathematics and enjoyed figuring out *gematrioth*.

"The amount of letters in our forefathers' and matriarchs' names is thirteen plus thirteen, which is twenty-six, and twenty-six is the *gematria* of the name of HaShem, His holy four-letter Name. Our first ancestors strove to bring HaShem into the world and to pass it on to their children and their children's children. We can remember these *gematrioth* — twenty-six and thirteen — every time we say in the *Shema 'HaShem echod.'* Really something, yeh, Sammy?"

"Wow, it's amazing, Jerry. But what does it have to do with Bar Mitzvah?"

"A lot. You'll see at Josh's Bar Mitzvah what I mean. It's no simple thing to bring the Oneness of HaShem into this world. It takes maturity and real commitment to stay true to Torah and mitzvoth; to keep our Yiddishkeit alive and well inside and out."

"What do you mean, 'inside and out'?"

"Oh, that's our battle with the *yetzer-harah*; outside, in the world of goyishkeit and inside, in our minds and hearts. But maybe I'll ask Dad to explain this idea to you since we're already home."

2 / The tug of war

⁂ Having finished supper, Mr. Goldstein was sitting in the kitchen, drinking a glass of ice tea while reading a *sefer*. When he heard the boys come into the house, he called out, "Jerry, have you boys finished packing for tomorrow's trip?"

"We sure have, Dad," answered Jerry as he walked from the hallway into the kitchen. "What time do we have to get up?"

"4:30."

"So early?" Sammy was surprised. "But the train doesn't leave until 7:15."

"No, Sammy," his father pointed to the train schedule on the table. "We made a mistake when reading the timetable. Really, the train is scheduled to leave at 6:15; so four-thirty isn't that early, especially since you also need time to *daven*. So don't forget to set your alarm."

"Okay."

"Dad," Jerry began as he sat down at the kitchen table, "Sammy and I were talking about the specialness of being thirteen and having a Bar Mitzvah. How would you explain about the *yetzer-harah* and the *yetzer-tov*?"

"I suppose you mean that before Bar Mitzvah a young person has only a *yetzer-harah* while from the day of the Bar Mitzvah onward he has also a *yetzer-tov*."

"Yeh."

"Well," began Mr. Goldstein, "First let's define our terms. The *yetzer-harah* is a force inside of us that seeks ways to have us do wrong. We know it has succeeded whenever we afterwards feel regret for having done or said something wrong. What makes us run out of the house without saying an after-beracha? The *yetzer-harah*. Or gets us angry even over unimportant matters? The *yetzer-harah*. It is part of our subconscious and a voice that confuses our proper decision-making.

"The *yetzer-tov*, on the other hand, is the voice of our conscience, which develops as our awareness develops. *Chazal* tell us that at the Bar Mitzvah, the *yetzer-tov* comes to us; it is called, in the *Zohar*, our new soul. From this time onwards, the power of making the right decisions is placed in our hands. Therefore, we are considered mature enough to handle all the *Taryag mitzvoth* and develop proficiency in them. This level of accountability is the sign of Jewish manhood and begins at the age of thirteen.

"Let me give you a *moshol* to help you understand the

transition from before the Bar Mitzvah when a young person has no *yetzer-tov* to after the Bar Mitzvah when he does have a *yetzer-tov*.

"Two rival armies are positioned on opposing hills with a large valley between them. They are both ready for battle. As long as the one is quiet and does not attack, the other is quiet too. However, once one side strikes out, the other side immediately counterattacks. Before the Bar Mitzvah, the *yetzer-harah* has no enemy to fight; so he does not have to use much strength to get his way. A child does most things out of impulse or simple motivations, such as reward..."

"And punishment," added Jerry as they all laughed.

"After the Bar Mitzvah, however, the *yetzer-harah* has an adversary to contend with, the *yetzer-tov*. Suddenly, the peaceful valley is alive with fierce fighting. New weapons are employed; attacks and counterattacks are made. The one-day war becomes two days, then three, then stretches into weeks, months, and years. A victory today leaves the enemy weak and humbled, but tomorrow he will be back in the valley again to try old, as well as new, tricks in this ceaseless warfare."

"But isn't it a little unfair," asked Sammy curiously. "It sounds to me like the *yetzer-tov* is on the losing side right from the very start. By the time it arrives on the scene, the *yetzer-harah* already has a thirteen-year head start."

"Yes, you're absolutely right, Sammy. Since the newborn *yetzer-tov* seems from the outset to be at a disadvantage, the battle front appears to be unbalanced. In fact, the contrast between them is expressed in the fourth chapter of *Koheleth*: 'Better is a poor and wise child than an old and foolish king.' *Chazal* explain that the 'poor child' represents the *yetzer-tov*.

It is called a child in relation to the *yetzer-harah* since, for thirteen years, the *yetzer-harah* alone has ruled as king.

"Now that the *yetzer-tov* is on the scene, the battle lines are set, but the balance of power is unequal. The *yetzer-tov* lacks counselors and loyal men in strategic positions; which to us means a perceptive awareness of right and wrong and an experienced capacity to reason out things accurately. Therefore, he is called 'poor.' The *yetzer-harah's* sovereignty stretches throughout all the 248 limbs; all his ministers and generals serve him well. In other words, we tend to let our natural impulses take over. And that, by the way, is why the *posuk* calls him 'foolish.' For example, being hungry is no excuse for poor behavior or missing out on a mitzvah. The *yetzer-tov's* sole source of power is his wisdom, as it says 'a poor *and wise* child,' and with it he saves the city and wins the war. And where does it get its wisdom? When the person learns the wisdom of Torah and really makes it a part of him."

Both Jerry and Sammy were listening intently to their father. Jerry nodded his head and asked, "Dad, is your description the famous battle of choice — *bechirah* — which we human beings are given?"

"Yes it is, Jerry. In English it's called 'free will.' "

"And aren't the lives of the twin brothers Yaakov and Esav a good example of the power of free will?" asked Jerry.

"Right again," answered Mr. Goldstein. "Indeed, the turning point in their lives came immediately after their Bar Mitzvah — right after they had received their *yetzer-tov* and had the *bechirah* to choose good or evil. Before then they both went to the same Talmud Torah and had more or less the same interests; after all, they were twins. After they turned thirteen,

Yaakov wanted to continue in yeshiva and develop his mind through the study of Torah and thereby rule over his natural impulses. Esav, on the other hand, chose to use his *bechirah* for other ends and let his impulses pull him here and there until, finally, he began visiting places of idol worship. He should have known better, but I guess he decided not to think deeply enough into his actions, especially the first, more innocent ones. Slowly, he got more and more used to his bad habits, and finally he convinced himself that what he was doing was right. Can you believe that! Well, the rest of the story of these two brothers is well known: one was worthy to become the father of the Twelve Tribes, and the other became Yisroel's worst enemy.

"The important thing to remember," continued their father, "is that the choice is placed in the hands of each person precisely at the time of his Bar Mitzvah. Also remember that when the choice is black and white, like don't turn on a light on Shabbat, it is easy to choose white. On the black and white score-card there is no battle; victory is already in hand. The battle front lies in the gray-color choices, the twilight area decisions of 'is it really bad?,' 'will anyone be the wiser?,' 'so what, it's only a little untrue.' *Bechirah* is the on-the-spot choice of what to say and how to act in life. It is our inner tug of war. This is what we were created for; to take up the battle and with the strength of Torah in us, to become the champions.

"The day of the Bar Mitzvah itself is very significant; it is the inauguration day of the 'poor but wise' *yetzer-tov*. Dovid *HaMelech* spoke about this day in the second chapter of *Tehillim*: 'The L-rd said to me, "You are My son; on this day I have given birth to you." ' The *Zohar* explains that when Dovid wrote, 'the L-rd said to me, "You are My son," ' he was describing his Bar Mitzvah, son of the mitzvoth. On this day he was a man, and it was as if he were reborn, as HaShem testified, 'on this day I have given birth to you.' It's like a new day of birth, for a young person has reached a new stage in life. No wonder he's so excited and..."

"And nervous," added Jerry, and everyone laughed.

3 / The 13-spoked wheel of faith

☙ Sammy thought for a moment and then remembered a question which he had before. "Dad, can you please tell me what do all of the *gematrioth* of thirteen have to do with the Bar Mitzvah?"

"Which ones?"

Jerry smiled. "Oh, I was telling Sammy about how the *gematrioth* of *echod* and *ahavah* are both thirteen and how each of them demonstrates the Oneness of HaShem."

"Yes," answered their father. "There are different ways of approaching the subject of Bar Mitzvah. *Gematrioth* like *echod* are a form of *drash* that help to establish the idea of Bar Mitzvah in a different dimension. For instance, the whole idea of Jewish manhood is to bring the Oneness of HaShem into the world through one's Torah study, *avodah* and good *midoth*. And this task begins as soon as a person has sufficient maturity."

"You mean like I don't object to emptying the trash anymore?" asked Sammy.

"Yes, that's a good example of your increasing sense of responsibility," nodded Mr. Goldstein.
"By the way, do either of you know why thirteen is the age of Jewish manhood?"

They stared at each other in silence.

"Most people," continued their father, "know that at thirteen one is fully responsible for all the mitzvoth, but they don't know where *Chazal* derived this rule from. No doubt this ignorance exists because we do not find any specific *posuk* telling us that thirteen — or any other age — is the transition between boy and man."

"Isn't the source from *Pirke Avoth*?" asked Jerry suddenly."Doesn't it say that at the age of five a boy begins studying *Chumash*, ten *Mishna*, and at thirteen he begins fulfilling the mitzvoth?"

"Yes, very good. That's a *Mishnaic* source. But what I'm really referring to are the *posukim* in the Torah on which this *Mishna* is based. Now the first one actually is in *Sefer Bemidbar*, 'When a man or woman shall commit any sin that men commit.' From here we see that only someone who is called *ish* [אִישׁ], man, or *isha* [אִשָּׁה], woman, is liable for his or her sins. And after going through the whole *Tenach*, we find that the minimum age of anyone referred to as an *ish* is thirteen. Where in the Torah is this reference? *Chazal* calculated that Levi, one of the sons of Yaakov *Avinu*, had just turned thirteen at the episode at Shechem, and the Torah calls Levi *ish*. Similarly, Bezalel who directed the building of the *Mishkan* in the desert is referred to as *ish*, and a lineage-chart of his father, grandfather, and great-grandfather shows that he was thirteen at that time."

Mr. Goldstein fingered his beard for a moment while he thought to himself. "You know, perhaps we can also find in the Rambam's Thirteen Principles of Faith special meaning for the young man who has just turned thirteen. After all, now he is beginning the journey in earnest, and this thirteen-spoked wheel of faith is essential for safe passage. Let's just read through them, and see what they mean. Jerry, please bring me the *Mishna Sanhedrin* with the *perush* of the Rambam."

Jerry returned from the living room and handed the *Mishna* to his father.

"Okay," began Mr. Goldstein as he flipped through the pages of the book until he came to the right place. "The first Principle says basically that *I believe with perfect faith that HaShem is the Creator and Guide of everything that has been created and that He alone has made, does make, and will make all things*. Not only did He create the distant stars and galaxies, the sun and moon, the seas and mountains, *but even* down to the millions of cells in our body, and the electrons that are whirling around inside them. Also included are the spiritual worlds outside the view of our reflecting telescopes and electronic microscopes. The *posuk*, by the way, which the Rambam bases this first principle on is from the Ten Commandments."

"I guess you mean, 'I am the L-rd your G-d,' " said Jerry.

"Right, and just as we are certain that this table exists,"

Mr. Goldstein banged on the table, "so we should be as strong in our *emunah* that the spiritual worlds exist."

"But where are these worlds?" asked Sammy. "I never saw them."

"Let me give you an example. The shoes a person wears reach up to the ankle, and boots go even higher. And extending up from the shoes are the legs and body of the person. *Chazal* compare a shoe to our body, our *guf*. Just as a shoe only covers a small part of the body, so also our *guf* only encases a small part of our soul. The soul, which is completely spiritual, extends way up to the highest heaven and only a small amount of it lives in our *guf*."

"I remember the teacher saying that everything has a spiritual counterpart, true?" posed Jerry.

"Yes, at one extreme, even a blade of grass has its own *malach* and, at the other extreme, corresponding to the Temple in Jerusalem, there is a spiritual *Beit HaMikdosh* in heaven."

After a short pause, Mr. Goldstein shifted himself in his chair and said, "Now let's continue with the second Principle. *I believe with perfect faith that the Creator is One, and that there is no oneness like His in any way; that He alone is our G-d, who was, is and will be*. Let's not confuse the Oneness of HaShem with other onenesses in the world. In the world of numbers, for instance, the number one symbolizes a single unit, yet it is followed by other numbers. Or people: each person is one, yet he is made up of many parts. Not so HaShem; His Oneness is absolute. Sammy, do you know which *posuk* the Rambam bases this one on?"

"Well, when I say the first *posuk* of the *Shema* it ends with *HaShem Echod* — HaShem is One."

"Sammy, I see that you're paying attention when you're praying. Very good. You know, boys, so much of our faith hinges on the *Shema* and the intense feelings it arouses in us when we say it."

"Maybe that's why HaShem wants us to say the *Shema* twice a day. Once a day just isn't enough," said Jerry.

"When saying the word *echod*," continued Mr. Goldstein, "we are supposed to be thinking a number of things."

"That He rules heaven and earth and the four directions of the world," declared Sammy, moving his hands as he mentioned each direction.

"Yes, that's true. In addition, we should be thinking that there is only one Creator and not two, *chas v'shalom*. By this I mean that when we look around us in the world everything has its opposite: light and darkness, holy and unholy, good and evil. We are not to think for one minute that these come from separate sources, *chas v'shalom*. The darkness, unholy and evil also come from *HaShem Echod*. And the reason for this we've already spoken about..."

"To open the door for *bechirah*," interjected Jerry.

"Well said, Jerry. Okay, now let's see number three: *I believe with perfect faith that HaShem is not a physical being, nor is He subject to physical changes; nor does He have any physical form whatsoever*. This means that since He has no body, He does not experience states of emotion, sleep, hunger, sickness, aging."

Sammy looked at his father from across the table. "But doesn't it say over and over again in the Torah things like 'the hand of HaShem' and that HaShem came down on *Har Sinai*?"

"Yes, that's a very good question, Sammy. All of these 'pictures' of HaShem are only used as a way of speaking for us to grasp His grandeur, might, and kindness; for Torah speaks the language of men. In fact, this subject is very, very deep, and when we have some more time we'll discuss it at greater length. For now, let's go on to the next one.

"The fourth Principle states that *I believe with perfect faith that HaShem is the first and the last*. First: even before the clock of time started ticking. Last: after *all* is said and done, He shall still be, forever and ever.

"Five: *I believe with perfect faith that it is appropriate to pray to Him alone, and that it is not proper to pray to any being besides Him*. Prayer unites us with HaShem. This is especially true when we tie together our thoughts, lips and heart. If our lips are saying *Shema Yisroel* while our hearts are thinking about an ice-cream sandwich, then ..."

"But it's hard to control our thoughts," sighed Jerry.

"Yes, it's hard, but that's our *avodah*. How proud we should feel to have a private audience with the King of Kings three times a day and to open our heart and soul to Him. *Davening* is no lip-service. It is a renewal of our love of HaShem.

"Moreover, prayer makes us honest with ourselves. That is why the word to pray, לְהִתְפַּלֵּל, means to judge oneself. Someone who thinks honestly about his actions and about the stirrings in his heart will realize that he has to be very humble before HaShem.

"Also," he said with a dramatic tone in his voice, "by

turning only to HaShem, we are standing up against all forms of idolatry."

"You mean," wondered Jerry, "that every time we *daven*, we are fulfilling the *posuk*, 'You shall have no other gods before Me'?"

"Most certainly!"

"But, Dad, what kind of idolatry is there today, anyway?" asked Sammy.

"First, Sammy, know that millions and millions of people still bow down to idols today. Second, many people think that idolatry refers only to certain ancient pagan religions that died out a thousand years ago and more. They are gravely mistaken. It happens that people are serving idols when they follow superstitions, such as not walking under a ladder or not letting a black cat cross their path. Moreover, some let astrological charts decide for them what to do and when to do it, and others join modern cults and such, and still others believe that 'Nature' runs the world. All of these are severing our eternal bond with HaShem. In a nutshell, then, anything which takes a person away from believing in HaShem and His Torah is the beginning of idolatry.

"Now let's see, where are we? Oh yes, the sixth Principle, which says *I believe with perfect faith that all the words of the prophets are true*. Imagine asking the Vilna Gaon how many words are in the Book of *Yehoshuah* or any other part of *Tenach*," wondered Mr. Goldstein. "Then ask him if even one word from all those tens of thousands of words is untrue. How do you think he would answer you?"

Sammy responded in a loud voice, "Of course he would say that they are all true."

NOW PLAYING
THE SAP!
WITH SUPERSTARS
MUSH HANDSOME And
FELICIA EYELASH
להבדיל
THE UNITED STATES OF AMERICA

"Without question," Mr. Goldstein continued. "The spirit of prophecy comes to a man who has reached the highest levels of self-perfection. How amazing it is to think that man — who is mortal and, therefore, must return his body to the earth — is granted the privilege of being given the words of HaShem directly. Of course, to become a *navi* of HaShem one must first be a true *tzaddik*."

"But hasn't HaShem taken away the power of prophecy?" asked Jerry.

"Yes. You're right, prophecy ended in the time of Nechemiah at the rebuilding of the second *Beit HaMikdosh*.

"This subject of prophecy is dealt with also in the next Principle,Principle number seven: *I believe with perfect faith that the prophecy of Moshe Rabbenu is true, and that he was the chief of all the prophets, both of those who preceded and of those who followed him*. Moshe's prophecy was incomparable to that of all other prophets — his was face-to-face. Actually, the Rambam points out four differences between Moshe Rabbenu and all the other prophets. First, only Moshe spoke directly to HaShem, and not through intermediary *malachim*. Second, other prophets received their prophecies while sleeping at night or day; Moshe's prophecies came to him while he was wide awake and standing up. Third, at the time of receiving the word of HaShem, Moshe felt neither fear nor any other physical weakness, whereas the other prophets did. And finally, only Moshe Rabbenu spoke with HaShem whenever he wanted.

"Next, the eighth Principle says *I believe with perfect faith that the whole Torah now in our possession is the same that was given to Moshe Rabbenu*. The *Sefer Torah* which we have today is the same one, word for word, as Moshe Rabbenu wrote down thousands of years ago. Moreover, you should know that Moshe did not write one word of the Torah from his own ideas; it all came directly from HaShem. In fact, anyone who denies even one part of the Torah by saying Moshe authored it himself, or that someone wrote historical events or moralistic stories or fables, *chas v'shalom* — such a person is denying the whole Torah.

"By the way, the words 'whole Torah' mentioned in this Principle also refer to the Oral Law, the *Torah she-baal-peh.*"

"That's really our work: when we study *Mishna* and *Gemora, Gemora* and *Mishna,*" smiled Jerry. "How the Torah *posukim* are explained and come alive with meaning!"

"Yes, when Rav Ashi and Ravina wrote down the *Gemora*, they were writing down what they had received from their *rebbeim* who in turn had received it from their *rebbeim* in a direct, unbroken chain all the way back to Moshe Rabbenu."

"I'm still curious," said Sammy as he turned a spoon in his hand. "Doesn't it say a lot of times in the *Gemora* that the *halacha* is like so-and-so. Did Moshe Rabbenu really teach the *Mishna* over by saying: 'Rabbi Akiva says... Rabbi Eliezer holds...Rabbi Meir says...'?"

"No, he didn't. The *nusach* in the wilderness was without the differences of opinions that we so commonly find in the *Mishna* of Rabbi Yehuda HaNassi's time. And the reason is simple: in every succeeding generation, little bits and pieces were forgotten and doubt arose as to the exact *halacha*. Different *rebbeim* held different opinions, each with a logical proof to support his position.

"In addition, sometimes things were so obvious in one

generation, but in the next they were not obvious anymore. The *Beit HaMikdosh* is one example. While it stood, many things were common knowledge — like the dimensions and functions of the buildings and the exact format of the *kohenim's* service. The generations after the destruction of the Temple, however, had a hard time figuring out what had been so clear and simple a hundred years before.

"So, to summarize, both parts of the Torah — written and oral — were handed down to Moshe at Sinai, and he transmitted them to Yehoshuah who passed them on to the next generation, and so on and so forth, generation after generation down to today."

"Yeh," said Jerry, "from *Zeide* to you, and from you to me, and from me to my kids, *im yirtzeh HaShem.*"

"You're right, Jerry, here there is no generation gap. Now let's go on to the ninth Principle. *I believe with perfect faith that the Torah will not be changed, and that there will never be any other Torah from HaShem.* Clothes fashions, for instance, change all the time, but not the structure of the human body. The *Sefer Torah* never changes, although its external enclosure — the *Aron Kodesh* — may look very different from the ones that existed in Rabbi Akiva's time. 'Never changes' means that nothing shall be added to it — even one letter more — nor taken away from it."

"Now I see why," commented Jerry, "that if even one letter is missing the whole *Sefer Torah* is *posul* and unusable."

"Absolutely, Jerry. It's good to see how principles come out into practical *halachoth*.

"Next, the tenth Principle says: *I believe with perfect faith that HaShem knows every action of men, and all their thoughts, as it says in Chapter 33 of Tehillim*, 'He who fashions their hearts alike; who considers all their deeds.' Yona tried to run away from HaShem. But even when Yona was in the belly of the fish, HaShem was listening to his thoughts, deep down there."

"How can HaShem hear everyone at the same time?" asked Jerry. "Don't we have a rule that even two simultaneous voices cannot be understood by one listener?"

"Yes, but that rule applies only to human beings. Man's brain can't receive two communications at the same moment. But not so *HaKadosh Baruch Hu*. For Him, as we said before in the third Principle, there is no question of easy or hard work, stress or sleepiness, or any human limitation.

"Next," Mr. Goldstein continued after a short pause, "the eleventh Principle says: *I believe with perfect faith that HaShem rewards those who observe His mitzvoth and punishes those who transgress them*. Let me tell you a story that *Chazal* relate concerning the reward of the righteous, from the *Gemora* in *Makoth*. Once Rabbi Akiva was traveling abroad with some other *chachamim* when they heard a roar coming from the city of Rome many miles away. Everyone began to cry, everyone but Rabbi Akiva. He began to laugh. 'Why are you laughing?' they asked in surprise. 'Why are you crying?' They explained, 'These people bow down to images and burn incense to idolatry while dwelling in safety and comfort. Our Temple, the House of G-d, on the other hand, has been burned down: should we not cry out?' Rabbi Akiva smiled sympathetically. 'This is just the reason why I am laughing. When I hear these idol worshipers, who are going against the will of HaShem — for even *Bnei Noach* are forbidden to serve idols — when I hear them enjoying themselves, I realize how great is the reward that is awaiting us — who do His will.' "

Sammy looked up at his father. "But, according to the Rambam, where do we see that HaShem punished the Romans?"

Mr. Goldstein thought for a moment. "Everybody knows the expression 'the rise and fall of the Roman Empire.' Note the wording 'and *fall*'; from this we understand that although the Romans may have enjoyed themselves and existed a long time, their apparent success was only to reward them in this world for any good acts which they did so that in the future world they would receive nothing. That is what Rabbi Akiva meant when he said, 'I realize how great is the reward that is awaiting us' — in the World to Come.

"Now let's see. The twelfth Principle says: *I believe with perfect faith in the coming of the* Moshiach, *and although he may tarry, even so I daily anticipate his coming.* Of course you know the famous story of the Chofetz Chaim. He always had a small suitcase by his bed with a Yom-Tovdic suit inside it. When asked what the suitcase was for, he replied, 'At any time the *Moshiach* may come, and I must be ready to go right away, having ready my best clothes for such an occasion.' "

"So when is he coming, Dad?" asked Sammy impatiently.

"Actually, the Rambam writes here that we are not to make calculations, interpreting verses in *Tenach* this way and that, and coming up with a date. The Rambam also states that the reason why he has so far not come is because we have not done *teshuva*. That is, we haven't fully humbled ourselves before HaShem. The remedy is placed in our hands..."

"Everybody just has to do *teshuva*!" proposed Jerry resolutely.

"Nowadays," continued Mr. Goldstein, "there are a number of yeshivoth for *baalei teshuva*, places where young men and women can get a true picture of Judaism, where all their questions can be answered and doubts removed, and where they can immerse themselves in Torah knowledge. It's an important turn in the right direction, a sign of things to come."

"So maybe things aren't so far away," said Jerry.

"Particularly," added Mr. Goldstein, "if we *frum* also remember that we have to do *teshuva*.

"And now for the thirteenth Principle: *I believe with perfect faith that there will be a resurrection of the dead at the time when HaShem desires it to be.* Absolutely everything is in HaShem's hands to do, even bringing a person back to life. The *Gemora* in *Sanhedrin* at the beginning of *perek Chelek* brings a number of hints from *Tenach* to the resurrection of the dead, as well as *kal v'chomers*. One of these hints is in a *posuk* we say every day in the *Shema*. Do you know which one I mean, Sammy?"

"Um, well I'm not sure..."

"At the end of the second *parsha* it says, 'That your days may be multiplied, and the days of your children, upon the land which HaShem swore unto your fathers to give them.' It doesn't say 'to give *you*'; it says 'to give *them*,' referring to our forefathers Avraham, Yitzchak and Yaakov. But we don't find that they were ever given *Eretz Yisroel*, and the Torah does say that they will receive it. So clearly, they must live again in order to fulfill the promise.

"I see here at the end of the Rambam's *perush*," Mr. Goldstein continued, "that he says quite emphatically that one should review the Thirteen Principles many times and think deeply into them. It is a good practice to recite them every day after *Shacharith*, especially since most *siddurim* have them listed at the end of *davening*. It is known that there are some *tzaddikim*, like the Sanzer Rebbe, who recited them more than once a day.

"I suppose that this is enough for one night," Mr. Goldstein said as he glanced at the clock on the wall. "It's almost ten o'clock! How time flies! And I suppose if you boys don't get yourselves off to bed in the next few minutes, no alarm clock in the world is going to get you up tomorrow morning, especially you, Sammy."

"Oh, you don't have to worry about me," grinned Sammy as he got up from his chair. "I'm a light sleeper, you know."

"Mother packed some sandwiches and fruit for you to take tomorrow on the train. Let's not forget them. Now go ahead upstairs and get ready for bed. Good night, boys."

"Good night, Dad," they both called out as they headed for the staircase. *B'ezrath HaShem*, we'll see you tomorrow morning."

4 / *The tailor-cut Bar Mitzvah suit*

"Come on, Sammy; hurry and get up. You don't want to miss the train, do you? We have to *daven*, and we still have to get last-minute things ready."

But it was 4:30 Thursday morning, and from Sammy's vantage point in his comfortable bed, he could not imagine rushing to catch anything. Besides, what a lovely dream he was having: opening Bar Mitzvah presents piled up all the way to the ceiling.

Dream world, real world. Wait a minute! That's right, thought Sammy. Today's the big day. We're off to Josh's Bar Mitzvah in New York. Wow! How could I be so silly and forget something so important.

"Umm," cracked Sammy's boyish voice, "*Modeh ani*

lifanecha..." As he washed his hands with *negel vasser* and began getting dressed, Sammy started thinking that in only six months he would be waking up to his own Bar Mitzvah day. The conversation with his father and brother last night had made a deep impression on him. But he wondered: how could this transformation into a full *eved HaShem* be accomplished with not so very much time remaining? And then he remembered the conversation which he had had only a few days ago with his *haftorah* teacher, Rabbi Adler, after his lesson had finished.

"I understand your problem," Rabbi Adler had said. "It's not easy to become a Jewish adult overnight. Really, though, it's a process which takes time and effort. But that crucial day — when you put on tefillin and wear your new suit and give your Bar Mitzvah *drash* — will give you a very big boost in the right direction. In addition, something very important which some people forget is to *daven* to HaShem that He should help us become full-fledged, G-d-fearing, *Yiden*.

"I'll tell you even better. There have been great Torah scholars and *tzaddikim* who in their youth were not successful in their studies. People thought of them as wild and unruly, not the most likely candidates for Torah greatness. However, when they turned thirteen years of age, they changed their old ways and started on the path of goodness and sincerity. It was a surprise and a delight to everyone. As they matured, the light of their saintliness and Torah learning began to shine, and some of them even became leaders of the generation. And do you know what helped a lot? *Davening*.

"Yes, indeed, in fact, there's this interesting story about the *tzaddik* Rebbe Elazar, the son of the Noam Elimelech, which I just have to tell you."

"But Rabbi Adler," Sammy had interrupted, "my mother told me to pick up some rye bread and something for dessert on the way home."

"Don't worry. This story won't take long, and the bakery will still be open.

"Anyway, as a boy, Reb Elazer was quite mischievous. He found it difficult to sit and learn and often refused to listen to his teachers, missing classes without permission on more than one occasion. When his saintly father was told of his son's behavior, he reacted patiently, occasionally responding, 'Let's wait until the day of his Bar Mitzvah.'

"So it happened. Not long before the Bar Mitzvah, his father, Rebbe Elimelech, asked a tailor to come to his house and bring the finest silk material for his son's Bar Mitzvah suit.

" 'Cut out the material in my presence,' Rebbe Elimelech told the tailor. 'But before you cut out each piece, tell me which section you are about to cut.'

"The tailor spread the fabric on the table and began carefully outlining with chalk the different sections. When he was ready to cut for the shoulder area, Rebbe Elimelech said to him, 'Repeat after me: I am cutting the shoulder pieces for Elazar. May all of his bodily movements be in the service of the Creator, may He be blessed.' Similarly, before cutting out the arm sections and the pants, the tailor repeated, 'I am cutting these out for Elazar. May he use his arms and legs only in the service of the Creator, may He be blessed.' And so it followed with each section: Rebbe Elimelech gave the instructions with the prayer, and the tailor repeated after him. Only then did the tailor cut the material."

"On the day of the Bar Mitzvah, Reb Elazar went and bathed specially for the occasion. Afterwards, his father helped him get dressed in the new suit. As they went to shul to *daven* and lay tefillin, everybody gazed at the young Elazar with wonder and amazement. He was all aglow, a new person altogether. He was *Rebbe* Elazar!

"He matured quickly and excelled at his studies, learning with ease *Mishna, Gemora* and the *Shulchan Aruch*. He set his mind and heart to his studies. A difficult Tosefoth was also difficult for him, but now he had the perseverance to analyze it carefully and review it again and again until it became clear. His astonishing progress was a mystery to everyone — to everyone, that is, except his father and the tailor who made his Bar Mitzvah suit. You see, Sammy, prayer has more power than people realize."

"Oh, really, Rabbi Adler, I never thought of it that way."

"It's important to pay attention to *every* detail. In fact, now that I think about it, what about tefillin? Have you started learning the laws of how to put them on?"

"Well, ah,... actually, to be truthful, I haven't thought much about it, yet."

"I understand," Rabbi Adler said sympathetically. "There is still quite some time before your Bar Mitzvah."

"Yes. Around six months."

"Good. But you should know that the laws of tefillin are quite complicated. If you want my suggestion, it would be a good idea to get started early."

"Okay," nodded Sammy.

"Well," Rabbi Adler had said as he had reached over to a nearby bookcase and had taken down a pamphlet. "I have this handbook on tefillin which I can lend you. It's based on questions and answers. Here, take it and start learning."

"Thanks. I sure will."

"By the way," Rabbi Adler had continued, "we see that working on the Bar Mitzvah *drash* strongly influences a person to feel the new horizon of adulthood which lies before him. Writing it out, checking up sources, working it over with his father or rabbi, preparing to speak publicly — all this, weeks if not months before the Bar Mitzvah celebration — opens up a new road before him."

"I'm nervous just thinking that I'll have to give a *drash*."

"That's a good sign, Sammy. Then you'll surely put your best efforts into it. Indeed, by preparing your *drash*, you'll see how to prepare all your learning. Check every step if it is based on solid reasoning. Then see if the steps fit together in a logical sequence. Good preparation is one of the best ways of making a real acquisition of your learning."

"But do you think that reaching Bar Mitzvah will be any easier if someone had tried to be a good student all the time?"

"What do you mean!" Rabbi Adler had replied. "Someone like yourself who takes his studies seriously will have much more ability to grow into a Torah Jew.

"In fact, I'm sure you remember the first *Mishna* in *Pesachim* which says: 'On the eve (*ohr* אוֹר) of the fourteenth day of Nisan we search the house for *chametz* by candle (*ner* נֵר) light.' Well, there's another way to read it to show a young person's entrance into manhood. At the beginning of his fourteenth year, the *yetzer-tov* enters him. Using the *ohr* (אוֹר)

of Torah and the *ner* (נֵר) of mitzvoth, נֵר מִצְוָה וְתוֹרָה אוֹר, he is now able to search out and remove the *chametz* within him, that is, the *yetzer-harah*. Moreover, the *ohr* (אוֹר), his Torah learning, which he achieved from before the beginning of his fourteenth year (*ohr l'arba esreh*) will enable him to be better prepared as he begins his search.

"Indeed," Rabbi Adler had continued enthusiastically, "being a respectful and diligent student is the perfect way to begin the road of Bar Mitzvah. With this time of their lives in mind, our righteous *chachamim* sang praise at the *Simchat Beit HaShoevah* in the *Beit HaMikdosh*: 'Happy are we that our youth has not brought us to shame in our old age!' Behaving properly now saves a Jew from being shamefaced when he reaches old age. Moreover, developing in his youth good habits of Torah observance, for instance, praying with *kavannah*, will serve him in good stead throughout his life. As Shlomo *HaMelech* explained in the Book of Proverbs: 'Train a young person in the way to go, and when he is old he will not depart from it.' Success in the future depends on decisions made now, Sammy. Full growth as a Jew means righteous behavior all the way from the beginning."

"Sammy, Sammy," called Jerry loudly, shaking Sammy from his thoughts. "Let's get moving. I'm going downstairs to *daven* now. You'd better get on the move and come downstairs right away."

"Okay," answered Sammy hurriedly, "I was just thinking, but now I'm all set to get going."

5 / *A special Bar Mitzvah gift*

Jerry and Sammy were at the Baltimore train station twenty minutes before the 6:00 A.M. express was due to leave. Their father had driven them to the station and quickly bought them their tickets. He and their mother would be driving up to New York the next day, *erev* Shabbat, and the whole family would return together Monday morning after the Bar Mitzvah celebration. The brothers were so excited about getting on the train and looking for just the right seats that they nearly forgot to say good-bye to their father.

"Be sure not to forget your luggage when you get off," called their father after them. "And don't forget to give Mother a call once you get to your cousin's house."

"Okay, Dad!" Jerry called back from the train window while Sammy waved good-bye. "Sure, we won't forget. See you tomorrow afternoon, *b'ezrath HaShem*."

A few minutes later the train was rolling slowly out of the

station, and the boys were happily seated in their seats.

"Well, Sammy, we made it."

"We sure did. Baruch HaShem," answered Sammy with a smile.

The train was rocking back and forth as it began to pick up speed. The streets of the city were just beginning to wake up and come to life. Suddenly, Jerry turned to his brother.

"Oh, no Sammy, do you know what I forgot? Oh, no! I don't believe it."

"What?"

"I forgot my tefillin!"

"Are you sure, Jerry? Maybe it's in your bag."

Jerry was already looking through his overnight bag, hoping that he would find his tefillin.

"I had everything neatly packed before going to sleep last night," Jerry explained. "Only my tefillin I left out so that I would have them to *daven* with this morning. But in all the last minute rush I simply forgot them. Would you believe that! They're probably still on my chest of drawers."

"Now," Sammy cheered up his brother, "you won't forget to call Mom and Dad when we get to the Katz's, will you? They will bring your tefillin with them tomorrow when they come up. So you see, there is nothing to worry about."

"You're right," muttered Jerry. "But all the same, it's my tefillin and my responsibility to take care of them. Besides, I need them for *davening* tomorrow morning."

"You can always borrow a pair. No?"

"You're right, but still it's not the same. My tefillin are like a part of me."

Sammy's curiosity was aroused. What, he thought to

himself, makes tefillin *that* special that they become part of a person. Of course, everyone knows that they are beautiful and holy and expensive. But so are a lot of other things, too.

The train was already speeding along the Maryland countryside. Sammy gazed out the window but was still thinking about the specialness of tefillin and wondering what it would be like when he would begin wearing his own pair. His father had ordered a set for him from a relative in New York over a year ago, and on Sunday his father planned to pick them up. Sammy was excited even though it would be five more months before he would start wearing them, about a month before his Bar Mitzvah.

Just the other night, his father had told him the true story of another young Jew's adventure in getting his first pair of tefillin. It was called "The Seraf's Bar Mitzvah gift."

The saintly Rebbe Uri of Stralisk was universally known as the "Seraf," because of the fiery enthusiasm of his prayers. His father had passed away when he was very young, and he was raised by his mother, a very pious woman, who earned a meager income as a seamstress. She well recognized her son's greatness and, even several years before his Bar Mitzvah, was concerned about the purchase of his tefillin.

She explained to young Uri: "I certainly understand your desire to have the finest, most carefully made tefillin. But now we don't have the money for such an expensive pair. Therefore, I suggest that every day I give you a few coins which you will save in a jar. The small amount of money will slowly add up, and *b'ezrath HaShem*, by the time of your Bar

Mitzvah there will be enough for you to buy the best tefillin."
And so it was. Day by day, coins were added, and the young Reb Uri happily watched the jar become more and more full.

At that time, there lived the well-known Rebbe Moshe of Peshevarsk. A very humble man, he was recognized throughout the world as an excellent tefillin-maker. Since the tefillin which he made were considered among the very finest, Reb Uri yearned whole-heartedly to be able to buy his pair from the holy Rebbe Moshe.

A few weeks before Reb Uri's Bar Mitzvah, there was just barely enough money in the jar to buy a set of these special tefillin. His mother exchanged the heavy coins for paper bills and carefully sewed them into the lining of his coat. With her blessings, Reb Uri eagerly set out by foot on the long journey to Peshevarsk, hoping to find wagon rides on the way. As it happened, no wagons were going in his direction, and he was forced to walk the whole distance. His only thought as he pushed onward was to reach Rebbe Moshe's home before his birthday and, thereby, be able to wear his new tefillin on the day of his Bar Mitzvah.

On the night of his Bar Mitzvah, Reb Uri was still a half-day's journey away from his destination. Should he rest the night and, setting out at dawn, reach Peshevarsk at midday? Or should he wend his way along the dirt road all night long and then try to find Rebbe Moshe first thing in the morning? His sole desire was to wear the holy tefillin on his arm and on his head the very first thing in the morning. Oh, how the longing burned inside of him! Even if Rebbe Moshe did not have a pair to sell him, he thought, at least perhaps he could borrow a pair from him. Reb Uri decided to push on. He walked the whole night, keeping awake by humming his favorite tunes and concentrating on the beautiful tefillin that he would be wearing, *im yirtzeh HaShem*, in a few more hours. By morning, he reached the city of Peshevarsk.

He asked where Rebbe Moshe the tefillin-maker lived and was directed to a narrow lane off the main street. He found the *sofer's* house and knocked at the front door. A tall, middle-aged man with a long, gray beard opened the door and motioned for him to come in. Even before Reb Uri could open his mouth to speak, Rebbe Moshe walked straight to the cabinet along the far wall and took out a deluxe pair of tefillin and handed them to him.

"Here!" explained Rebbe Moshe. "Take this pair of tefillin that I have already prepared for you. I've been waiting for you to come."

Reb Uri was speechless. He started to open up the lining of his coat in order to pay the tefillin-maker, but immediately Rebbe Moshe stopped him and utterly refused to take any money for the tefillin.

"It is a gift for your Bar Mitzvah," he said with a kindly smile.

Reb Uri's joy was boundless; tears of gratitude rolled down his cheeks. Rebbe Moshe began explaining some of the deeper principles of tefillin as he carefully laid them on the new Bar Mitzvah man. Immediately, Reb Uri felt a great and wondrous holiness surround him, for now he was a man, armed to do the holy work of the Jew in this world.

Sammy was sure that the tefillin which his father was buying would also make him feel special. He remembered his teacher once telling the class that the more one knows about tefillin, the more meaningful is the experience of putting them on and *davening* with them. To know this mitzvah of tefillin well is very important, for it is compared to all the other mitzvoth. Moreover, it is a daily example of the Torah Jew's complete acceptance of the Oral Tradition (*Torah she-baal-peh*), the essential partner of the Written Law (*Torah she-bichtav*). For the Written Law tells us very little about tefillin; indeed, it is the Oral Tradition alone that tells us what tefillin are, how to make them, when to wear them, and so on.

Now Sammy was beginning to feel sorry that he had not studied more about tefillin. In just a few more hours, he would be meeting his cousin Joshua, and it would have been exciting to ask him good questions about tefillin. After all, tefillin is *the* mitzvah of the Bar Mitzvah young man.

"Wait a minute," said Sammy aloud. "Maybe I brought along the tefillin handbook which my *haftorah* teacher lent me. It could be together with some of the books I threw into my travel bag to read on the trip." And he immediately started going into his hand baggage.

"What did you say?" asked Jerry.

"Oh, my *haftorah* teacher lent me a book," muttered Sammy, with his head lowered below the seat, "and maybe I have it with me. Now, here's my *Chumash* and also... let me see if...Oh, great, it's here."

"What's here?" asked Jerry. But Sammy was so preoccupied as he pulled out "The Tefillin Handbook" that Jerry realized that now was no time for conversation.

Sammy first read the opening questions in the handbook and then carefully studied the answers, using the accompanying diagrams to clarify his understanding.

6

THE
TEFILLIN
HANDBOOK
A Practical Guide
based on Talmudic sources
and the Mishna Berura

edited by Shimon Hurwitz

graphics by Shmuel Gluck (and Craig Ehrlich)

photography by Donn Gross, D.R.

illustration by I.A. Kaufman

copyright © 1984 by David Rossoff

All rights reserved. No part of this book, including the graphic art and photographs, may be reproduced in any form without written permission from the author.

Contents

Dear Rabbi Rossoff נ״י,

I have received your booklet on Tephilin, which has already been recommended by Rabbinical Authorities in Jerusalem. I have read it through, and I feel sure the English speaking public will derive great benefit from this handbook which I strongly recommend.

You have succeeded to explain in simple language the essence of the Mitzvah, and through accepting advice from Rabbis in all doubtful cases, you have assured yourself בע״ה that you will succeed in your motives.

I feel sure that your booklet will impress on readers the importance to lay Tephilin every day, and to observe the Mitzvah according to the Laws as set up in *Shulchan Aruch*.

Accept my blessings, you should succeed in your work as through the Mitzvah of Tephilin we will sanctify the name of G-d and be blessed with complete redemption.

Best Wishes
Moishe Sternbuch

RABBI MOSES FEINSTEIN
455 F. D. R. DRIVE
New York, N. Y. 10002

Oa
ORegon 7-1222

משה פיינשטיין
ר"מ תפארת ירושלים
בנוא יארק

בע"ה

הנה קבלתי הקונטרס על הלכות תפילין שחיברו הרה"ג מוהר"ר דוד רוסאף שליט"א. קונטרס זה נכתב באנגלית, ומסרתיו לנכדי, הרה"ג מוהר"ר מרדכי טנדלר שליט"א, שעיין בו, ושיבחו כספר שיכול להיות לתועלת לאלו שמתחילים ללמוד הלכות אלו, מאחר שנכתב בלשון בהיר ונסדר באופן משכלת. והספר כולל גם מראה מקומות ארוכות, שיעיין בו אלו שרוצים להעמיק יותר בהלכות אלו.

והריני מברך להמחבר הנ"ל שיצליחהו השי"ת בספרו זה, ויזכה ע"י להרבות ידיעות התורה.

ועל זה באתי על החתום בכ"ד אדר שני שדמ"ת בנוא יארק.

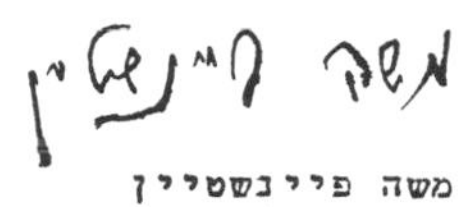

משה פיינשטיין

I received the booklet on the laws of *tefillin* written by David Rosoff. As this booklet is written in English, I gave it to my grandson, the learned Rabbi Mordechai Tendler, who examined it, and praised it as a work that can be useful to persons beginning to learn these laws, since it is written in clear language and arranged in an intelligent manner. The work includes lengthy references as well, which will be of interest to those who wish to delve further into these laws.

I hereby bless the author, that HaShem may give him success with this work; and may he be privileged to increase by it a knowledge of the Torah.

To this I have set my name, on 24 Adar II, 5744, in New York.

Vaad Mishmereth Stam

ועד משמרת סת"ם

*The center for international activities to preserve and promote the halachic integrity of scribal arts: Torah **S**crolls, **T**efillin **A**nd **M**ezuzos*

Rosh Chodesh Teveth 5744

How truly pleased and happy we are at seeing the new publication, **The Tefillin Handbook**, the fruitful work of Rabbi David Rossoff, שליט"א, who has worked diligently and tirelessly to bring merit to the Jewish people through this important book, as it is testified to by great rabbinical authorities in their recommendations.

Concerning STAM, in general, and mitzvath tefillin, in particular, as great as their lofty holiness and as cherished as they are to our people, unfortunately there is no measure to the fraudulent pitfalls which exist in this holy area. Many people throughout the world are being misled, as it is known, "the greater the holiness, the greater the likelihood of destroying such holiness." The problem applies not only to the *halachoth* of proper writing and formation of the letters, whose *kashruth* is by a hairbreadth, but also to other important *halachoth* of tefillin such as *batim, retzuoth*, proper binding on the arm and head, and so forth.

From experience, we are certain that our fellow Jews wear tefillin with the sole desire of performing the mitzvah as required but fail in this goal simply because they lack sufficient knowledge of the *halachoth*. And, therefore, it is fitting to give respect and esteem to the author, Rabbi David Rossoff, who felt impelled to deal with this important mitzvah. And how great is his merit (see *Sefer Chassidim*, section 65), because increasing the knowledge of these *halachoth* will promote the diligence and carefulness with which this mitzvah is performed and, thereby, will remove great disgrace from the Jewish people.

In this merit, may we be deserving of all the Torah blessings and promises that are mentioned concerning the mitzvah of tefillin, and may we see fulfilled in us, as it is stated, "And all the peoples of the earth will see that the Name of Hashem is called upon you and they shall be in awe of you."

בברכת התורה

4902 16th Avenue, Brooklyn, N.Y. 11204 Phone: (212) 438-4963

PREFACE

Tefillin has the potential to bind body and soul to the Creator. But as a minimum, we must fulfill one essential condition: that we know we are putting on tefillin. If this prerequisite is not fulilled, the tefillin become no more than "boxes of stone," *chas v'shalom* (see *Aterath Zekenim* 25:2).

Therefore, in order both to assist the novice and to provide a quick review for others, this handbook has been prepared for the benefit of the Torah public.

In it, three areas of *hilchoth* tefillin have been tied together. First, the practical *halacha l'maaseh* is set down with its reference in the *Mishna Berura* and *poskim*. Second, the Talmudic source of the *halacha* is discussed side by side with the *halacha*. And thirdly, relevant stories and reasons for the *halacha* have also been included.

It is hoped that this "tripled-stranded cord" will help dispell areas of ignorance and make certain that we are wearing tefillin and not "boxes of stone."

THIRTEEN-POINT QUESTIONNAIRE

First we want you, our reader, to test your knowledge on tefillin, and then we will give the answers. Put a check by each question where you know the answer. After you finish this handbook, come back again and make sure that you know the answers to all the questions.

[1] What do the words "tefillin" and "*totofoth*" mean? What do they tell us about the meaning of wearing tefillin?
[2] How many times is the mitzvah of tefillin mentioned in the Torah? Where? Why?
[3] What is the difference in the order of the *parshiyoth* between Rashi and Rabbenu Tam?
[4] Why does a right-handed person bind tefillin on his left arm, and a left-handed person, on his right arm? Why is the *shel yad* placed on the biceps muscle of the arm and not, as the *posuk* says, "as a sign upon your *hand*"? (*Devorim* 6:8).
[5] Why do we place the *shel rosh* above the forehead and

not, as the *posuk* states, "as frontlets between your eyes"? (Ibid.)

[6] Why are tefillin perfectly square? Why must they be black? What material are they made from and why?

[7] Why does the *shel yad* have one compartment for all the *parshiyoth* while the *shel rosh* has four separate compartments?

[8] Why is the *shel yad* put on first and the *shel rosh* taken off first?

[9] How many *berachoth* are made? Must one stand when putting on tefillin?

[10] Are the straps of the tefillin absolutely necessary? Must they also be black? How many times is the strap wound around the arm? The permanent knots of the *shel rosh* and the *shel yad* look like which Hebrew letters?

[11] What are the *titura* and the *ma'abarta*?

[12] Can tefillin be worn at night? Why are they not worn on Shabbat and Yom Tov? When are tefillin first worn?

[13] Why is the letter *shin* found only on the *shel rosh?* How many times? Can it be simply painted on? Why does one *shin* have four heads?

ANSWERS WITH EXPLANATION

[1] WHAT DO THE WORDS "TEFILLIN" AND "TOTOFOTH" MEAN? WHAT DO THEY TELL US ABOUT THE MEANING OF WEARING TEFILLIN?

According to most commentators, the word "tefillin" comes from the Hebrew word *pilel*, [פליל], which can mean either to argue, "And Pinchas stood up and argued [ויפלל]" (*Tehillim* 106:30), or to think out clearly, as in the *posuk*, "I had not thought [פללתי] to see your face" (*Bereishith* 48:11).[1]

The word *totofoth*, referring to the tefillin *shel rosh*, means headband and is often translated "frontlets."[2]

In what ways do these definitions help us to understand better the mitzvah of wearing tefillin?

First, tefillin represent a visible proof and testimony to the world that the Name of HaShem is placed on the Jewish People. By publicly wearing these frontlets, for no other reason than to fulfill HaShem's commandments, we are dramatically arguing HaShem's absolute rulership. Thereby, we show ourselves as His only true and obedient servants, receiving the awe and respect due His representatives. This is the meaning of the *posuk*, "And all the peoples of the earth shall see that the Name of the L-rd is called upon you; and they shall be afraid of you."[3]

Second, tefillin tell us the central role of thinking in the Jewish way of life. Concentration, meditation, memorization are essential when the Jew prays and learns Torah.[4] The tefillin *shel rosh* shows the requirement of bringing the reasoning powers of the brain closer to the service of HaShem. The tefillin *shel yad* opposite the heart indicates the need for controlling passionate thoughts, for example, anger, greed, lust.

Third, tefillin remind us to *think* about our Divine mission in the world. The four *parshiyoth* inside the tefillin represent the four letters of HaShem's Name[5] and define four basic components of our Jewish existence:

(a)Total acceptance of the yoke of the Kingdom of Heaven [Love of HaShem].[6]

(b)Total acceptance of all the commandments of HaShem [Fear of HaShem].[7]

(c)Complete dedication of all material possessions to the service of HaShem [self-sacrifice].[8]

(d)Absolute realization that HaShem controls all of nature and the events of man [the Exodus from Egypt].[9]

Now we can understand why someone who recites the *Shema* without putting tefillin on is compared to a witness who gives false testimony.[10] For tefillin are the physical representation of the words which we are speaking and thinking about, and it would be false to mention the requirement of wearing tefillin and not put them on.

Fourth, we can also define tefillin in the sense of arguing or pleading our cause before HaShem.[11] "See that we are wearing tefillin and please accept our prayers – even if we have shortcomings. Our desire to do Your will is expressed at this very moment as we wear Your mitzvah of tefillin. So, though we ourselves may have no merits, may the tefillin plead [פליל] our cause and give us the merit to have our prayers answered."

[2] HOW MANY TIMES IS THE MITZVAH OF TEFILLIN MENTIONED IN THE TORAH? WHERE? WHY?

Tefillin are mentioned four times in the Torah:

1) קדש *Kadesh* (*Shemoth* 13:1-10).
2) והיה כי יביאך *V'haya ki yevi'acha* (Ibid. 13:11-16).
3) שמע ישראל *Shema Yisroel* (*Devorim* 6:4-9).
4) והיה אם שמע *V'haya im shamoah* (Ibid. 11:13-21).

These same four *parshiyoth* are placed in both the tefillin *shel rosh* and the tefillin *shel yad* as we partially discussed in the question before. The *Shema* and *V'haya im shamoah* we say in the *Kiriyath Shema* of *Shacharith*, and it is a good custom to say the other two, either right after putting on the tefillin or after *davening*, before removing the tefillin.[12]

The *Shema* describes the Oneness of HaShem and our desire to join with that Oneness even until death. This *parsha* is called "accepting the yoke of the Kingdom of Heaven" and is an intense expression of our undying love of HaShem. By studying

14 THE TEFILLIN HANDBOOK

Torah wholeheartedly, we form an inseparable closeness to HaShem, as it says, "...and you shall speak of them,"[13] that is, by constantly learning Torah the Oneness of HaShem will become more a part of you. Further, when we check through all the mitzvoth, we discover that tefillin more than any other mitzvah implants in us the full scope of learning Torah, as the *posuk* says, "so that the Torah of HaShem shall be in your mouth."[14]

Rabbenu Yona also explains that tefillin are an expression of our acceptance of the Almighty's Kingship since the *shel rosh* shows our willingness to submit our minds to Him, and the *shel yad* shows our willingness to subjugate our bodily actions to His will.[15]

While the *Shema* expresses the love of HaShem, *V'haya im shamoah* teaches fear of HaShem by describing the rewards for doing the mitzvoth and the punishments for failing to do them. Tefillin represent the obligation to fulfill *all* of HaShem's mitzvoth since many mitzvoth directly or indirectly relate to the mitzvah of tefillin – for example, studying Torah [the *Shema* must be read with tefillin on], eating kosher animals [only the skin of kosher animals may be used to make tefillin], and believing in the Oral Tradition [that the straps must be black] and the wisdom of *Chazal* [not to wear tefillin at night].

Further, we see in this *parsha* that the stress is changed from the singular to the plural in order to teach us that the Jewish community as a whole is also responsible for keeping HaShem's mitzvoth. How wonderful it is to see this joint responsibility in action when, for example, one Jew is helping another to put on tefillin!

The last two *parshiyoth, Kadesh* and *V'haya ki yevi'acha*, appear strange and unrelated to tefillin. What does redeeming the firstborn have to do with tefillin? How do the Exodus and the mitzvah of *Pesach* and the *Haggadah* fit into the mitzvah of tefillin? Rabbi Hirsch explains[16] that when the firstborn were set apart to act as priests of the Jewish People,[17] a misunderstanding might have occurred, namely, that just the firstborn were holy and not the rest of the Jewish People. Therefore, when Moshe gave over the mitzvah of the firstborn, he reminded everybody of the Exodus – which equally freed everybody from bondage and equally brought them all into freedom. Further, he mentioned the significance of transmitting the freedom to everybody – as we do by reading the *Haggadah* on the *Seder* night – which shows that everyone has an equal task in serving HaShem. Finally, Moshe taught them that the mitzvoth – exemplified by tefillin – sanctified everyone equally, but the firstborn were given the additional task of conducting the Temple service.

[3] WHAT IS THE DIFFERENCE IN THE ORDER OF THE *PARSHIYOTH* BETWEEN RASHI AND RABBENU TAM?

What is the order of the *parshiyoth*? Our first guess would be that they are the same order as they appear in the Torah. Indeed,

Rashi understands it that way (see Diagram 1). Rabbenu Tam, however, changes the last two around as can be seen in Diagram 1,[18] but he agrees with Rashi that when writing the four *parshiyoth*, the *sofer* must write them in the order in which they appear in the Torah.

DIAGRAM 1

3	4	2	1	RABBENU TAM
4	3	2	1	RASHI

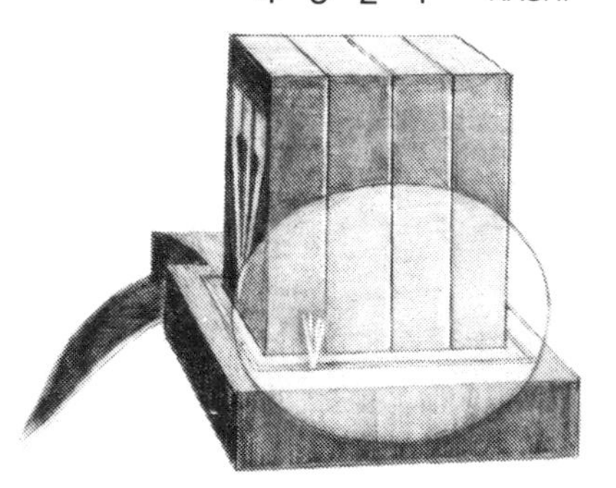

1 קדש
2 והיה כי יביאך
3 שמע ישראל
4 והיה אם שמע

PLACE WHERE CALF'S HAIR STICKS OUT
1 – ACCORDING TO RASHI
2 – ACCORDING TO RABBENU TAM

Today Rabbenu Tam tefillin are generally worn by Sephardim and Chassidim, but because of their high level of holiness, they are not worn until after marriage. Interestingly, some Chassidic groups have the *minhag* of wearing Rabbenu Tam already from the time of Bar Mitzvah. The *berachoth* are made only on the Rashi tefillin which are put on first and not on the Rabbenu Tam tefillin.

It is easy to recognize the *shel rosh* of Rabbenu Tam tefillin: look where the thread of calf's hair sticks out. The accepted *halacha* is that this hair should come out next to the compartment containing *V'haya im shamoah*.[19] Since Rashi and Rabbenu Tam disagree over which compartment *V'haya im shamoah* goes into, the calf's hair is located at a different place according to each viewpoint (see insert to Diagram 1).

[4] WHY DOES A RIGHT-HANDED PERSON BIND TEFILLIN ON HIS LEFT ARM, AND A LEFT-HANDED PERSON, ON HIS RIGHT ARM? WHY IS THE *SHEL YAD* PLACED ON THE BICEPS MUSCLE OF THE ARM AND NOT, AS THE *POSUK* SAYS, "AS A SIGN UPON YOUR *HAND*"? (*DEVORIM* 6:8).

When the Torah mentions "hand" without discriminating between right or left hand, it means the left hand. *Chazal* understood this principle because whenever a *posuk* refers to the right hand specifically, it says either "right" or "right hand," as in "Why do You withdraw Your hand, even Your right hand?" (*Tehillim* 74:11).[20]

Another way that *Chazal* explain that the *shel yad* is placed on the left hand is by comparing the *posuk* "you shall bind it as a sign" with the *posuk* that follows it, "...and you shall write it on your doorposts."[21] Just as writing is normally done with the right hand, so also the binding should be done with the right hand. Obviously, then, if the right hand is doing the binding, the tefillin must be placed on the left hand.

There is yet a third method to prove that tefillin are put on the left hand.[22] At the end of *V'haya ki yevi'acha* (*Shemoth* 13:16), "your hand" is spelled with an extra *hei*, יָדְכָה, normally used to show a feminine ending. Here it hints to "your weak(er) hand," which for a right-handed person means his left hand and for a left-handed person, his right hand.[23] Someone who uses both hands equally well, or who writes with one hand though his other hand is stronger, should consult his rabbi.

Now that we know the sources for placing it on the left arm, how do we know to place it on the biceps muscle between the shoulder and the elbow, and not on the forearm between the elbow and the wrist, or on the palm of the hand itself? The *Gemora* discusses the question: "The Academy of Menashe taught:[24] 'Your hand' refers to the biceps muscle." And how do we know this to be true? Rabbi Eliezer gives one explanation:[25] " 'And it shall be for *you* as a sign' – for you, and not for others." If a person wore tefillin on his hand, everybody would see it. However, if he wears tefillin on the upper part of his arm since his shirt would usually cover it, then it is a "sign" only for himself. The *halacha* is that the tefillin *shel yad* does not have to be covered so long as it is on the part of the arm which people normally cover.[26] Still, the better practice is always to cover the tefillin with one's shirt sleeve.[27]

Rabbi Yitzchak offers another method of learning where on the arm the tefillin should be placed.[28] The Torah says, "And you shall lay My words in your heart...and you shall bind them."[29] The binding of the *shel yad* shall be on the arm opposite the heart, that is, on the biceps muscle. From Rabbi Yitzchak's words, we learn that we should tilt the *shel yad* slightly towards the body so that when the arm hangs down, the tefillin (and its *yud*-shaped knot) will be directly opposite the heart[30] (see Diagram 2).

DIAGRAM 2

RIGHT

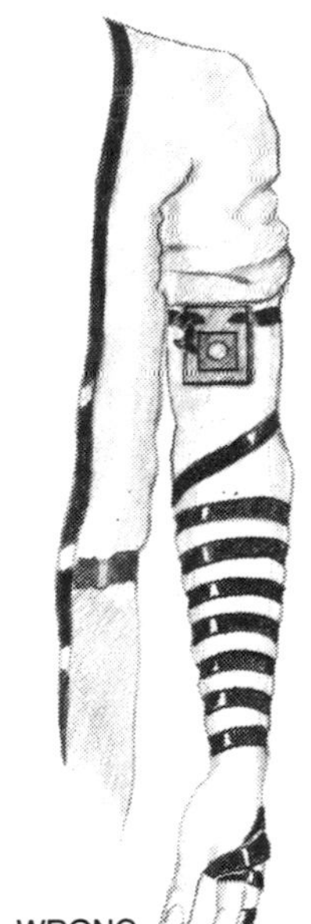

The upper part of the arm is divided roughly into three sections (see Diagram 3). The middle section is the area in which the muscle bulges and is known as the biceps muscle. The proper place for the *shel yad* begins at the *middle* of this area and continues along the bulge towards the direction of the elbow. Higher up than this bulge towards the shoulder should not be used, and very close to the elbow, which is already below the bulge of the biceps muscle, should also not be used.

DIAGRAM 3

However, when there is a wound or bandage on the biceps muscle, tefillin are not allowed to be placed on the bandage but must instead be placed either just below the biceps muscle or, if this area is also wounded, just above the biceps muscle.[31] If these areas also cause discomfort, a rabbi should be consulted whether the *shel yad* is still required.

Although some authorities do not view the tefillin straps as a separation between the tefillin and the flesh of the arm, it is better not to wind the strap under the *bayith* of the *shel yad*.[32]

Why did the Torah seemingly mislead us concerning the proper place for the *shel yad*? In fact, we are warned that anyone who follows the literal words and wears tefillin on the palm of his hand is considered a denier of the Oral Law.[33]

Chazal tell us that the key to fulfilling the mitzvoth is *not* to follow blindly the apparent simple meaning of the written word.[34] Instead, the *Torah she-baal-peh*, which was given hand-in-hand with the Written Law on *Har Sinai*, is our life-line to truth. Therefore, those who do not accept the teaching of our *chachamim* who received it in a direct chain from Moshe Rabbenu are cutting off this life-line and deny our most basic principles. Tefillin affirm our belief in the Oral Tradition and the *chachamim* who conveyed it from the generations before to our own generation.

[5] WHY DO WE PLACE THE *SHEL ROSH* ABOVE THE FOREHEAD AND NOT, AS THE *POSUK* STATES, "AS FRONTLETS BETWEEN YOUR EYES"? (*DEVORIM* 6:8).

Chazal teach that the correct position of the tefillin *shel rosh* is *completely* on the hair at the front of the head and extends

22 THE TEFILLIN HANDBOOK

backward about half the length of the head.[35] We fulfill the requirement that the tefillin be "between your eyes" by being certain to center it in the middle of the head, directly *above* the point between the eyes (see Diagram 4).

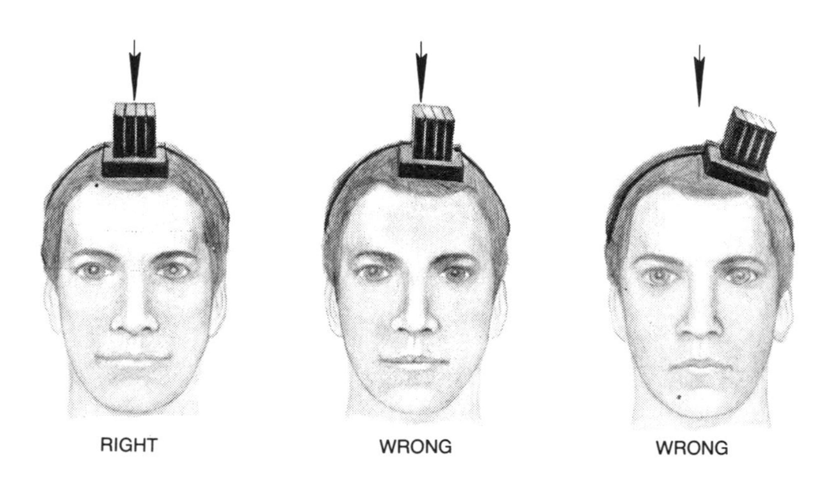

DIAGRAM 4

Chazal explain that the tefillin *shel rosh* is not placed directly between the eyes because of a *gezerah shava*, a comparison of laws based on the same wording in two places.[36] The words "between your eyes" appear in *Devorim* 14:1 where the prohibition against making a baldness between your eyes is mentioned. Making a baldness as a sign of mourning refers to pulling out the hair on the top of the head. From here, therefore, we understand that with tefillin the expression "between your eyes" means the place on the top of the head.

Special care should be taken to be sure that the *shel rosh* is always in its proper place.[37] Some people use a small pocket mirror to check if the tefillin is perfectly centered while others will ask a friend to see if their *shel rosh* is correctly positioned.[38] It is highly recommended to touch both the *shel yad* and the *shel rosh* regularly, except during the *Shemone Esre,*[39] in order that you should not forget that you are wearing tefillin [היסח הדעת].[40] With your right hand, first touch the *shel yad* and then the *shel rosh*. Further, during the *Kiriyath Shema*, touch the *shel yad* when saying "You shall bind them for a sign on your hand" and the *shel rosh* when saying "as frontlets between your eyes."

There is a famous story in the *Gemora* that took place during a discussion on the tefillin *shel rosh.*[40a] Pilimo asked Rabbi Yehuda HaNassi: "On which head does a two-headed man put on tefillin?" Rebbi was upset at such an absurd question. "Either you leave my presence and go into exile," he ordered, "or else consider yourself under a ban of excommunication." At that moment, a man entered the yeshiva to ask a question regarding the redemption of his firstborn son. "My wife just gave birth to a baby boy with two heads. How many shekel coins do I have to give to the kohen, five as the Torah commands because he is one child, or ten, that is, five for each head?"

Actually, Pilimo was asking a very basic question concerning our *Avodath HaShem*: what parts of our complex mind are we to bring into the service of HaShem?[41] The two heads represent two types of thoughts, one worldly and one heavenly. Pilimo wanted to know if while wearing tefillin a person has both worldly and heavenly matters on his mind, which one should he subjugate to HaShem? Rabbi Yehuda HaNassi reacted sternly because to him the answer was obvious – both types of thoughts have to be turned completely over to the service of HaShem.

The *Mishna Berura* (*Orech Chaim* 27:9 [33]) writes that many people are mistaken about the correct position of the *shel rosh* and say that the edge of the *bayith* (that is, the *ma'abarta*)[42] must touch the hair-line, but the *bayith* itself should lie on the forehead between the eyes. They, in fact, are the ones who are not fulfilling any mitzvah at all. Therefore, one should be extremely careful that all the *bayith*, including the *titura*[42] (base), lies on the hair of the head (see Diagram 5). And best of all, continues the *Mishna Berura*, is to place it slightly further back on the head away from the hair-line to guard against it accidentally sliding forward onto the forehead.

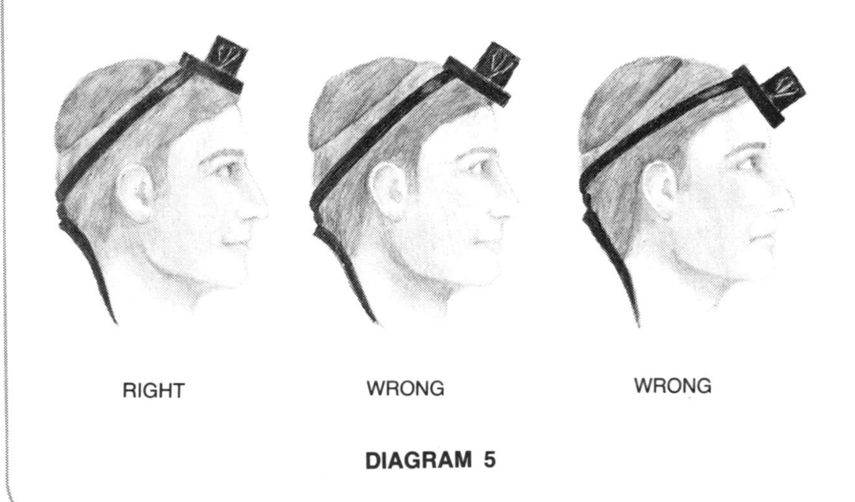

RIGHT WRONG WRONG

DIAGRAM 5

A person whose hair-line forms a "widow's peak" must move his tefillin back far enough so that all of it rests on his hair and not part on his hair and part on his forehead (see Diagram 6).

WIDOW'S PEAK

RIGHT

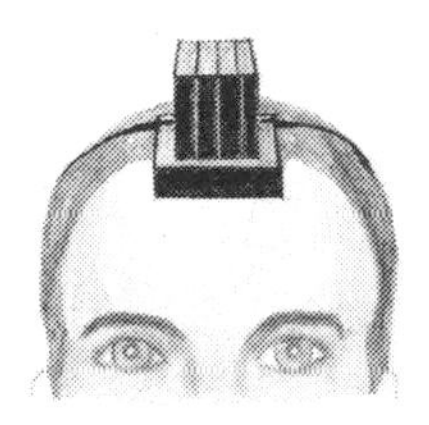

WRONG

DIAGRAM 6

Hair which slopes down slightly onto the forehead does not make the forehead a "free parking zone" for the *shel rosh*. The hair-line is determined by the roots of the hair and not its ends. In addition, long locks of hair lift the tefillin up away from the scalp and cause two problems.[43] First, it is more difficult to keep the *shel rosh* set exactly in the middle of the head because it is resting on an unstable layer of thick hair. And second, some authorities hold that such hair is a separation between the tefillin and the head since it cannot be claimed that long hair is its natural length. Practically speaking, someone with long hair should at least brush the hair down and not backward in order to avoid this problem.[43a]

The *shel rosh* is also called by the name *kanfe yona* (dove wings) because of the famous story that happened to Elisha.[44] The wicked Roman Empire forbade – on penalty of death –

anyone from wearing tefillin. The decree, however, did not alter Elisha's serving his Creator, and he continued wearing his tefillin even publicly. Once, when a Roman officer saw him with his tefillin on, Elisha ran away as the officer chased after him. When Elisha realized that he was going to be overtaken by the officer, he stopped and took off his *shel rosh* and held it tightly in his hand.

"What's that in your hand?" snarled the officer viciously.

Elisha stood his ground and simply replied, "Kanfe yona."

"Let me see," ordered the Roman.

Elisha stretched forth and opened his hand, revealing a dove.

For this reason he was called Elisha *Baal Kanfayim* ("Elisha, the possessor of wings").

(See Photographs, p.34 for three *kanfe yona* ways of wrapping the straps of the *shel rosh*.)

[6] WHY ARE TEFILLIN PERFECTLY SQUARE? WHY MUST THEY BE BLACK? WHAT MATERIAL ARE THEY MADE FROM AND WHY?

Halacha l'Moshe m'Sinai requires that both the *shel yad* and the *shel rosh* be perfectly square. This rule applies to both the *titura* (base) and the stitching that uses twelve holes which, when sewn together, hold the bottom flap of the *titura* flush against the top flap (see Diagram 10).

To ensure that a perfect square is made, the two diagonals (A–A, B–B) must be identical in length and at 90° angles, thereby making the sides of the *titura* (A–B, B–A) equal to each other (see Diagram 7).

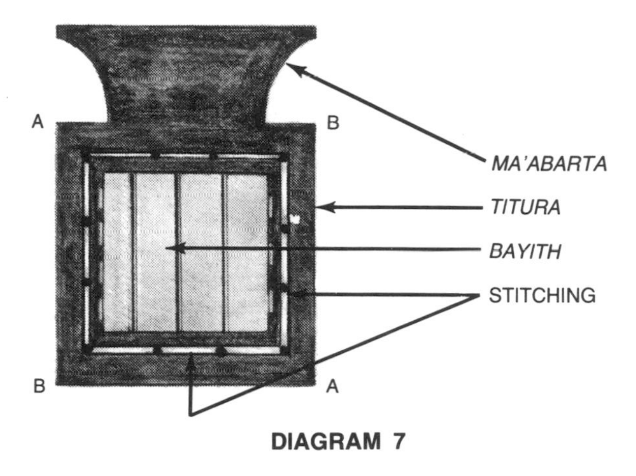

DIAGRAM 7

The sides of the *bayith* (see Diagram 8, a–b) also must be square, but its height (c) does not have to be the same length. In

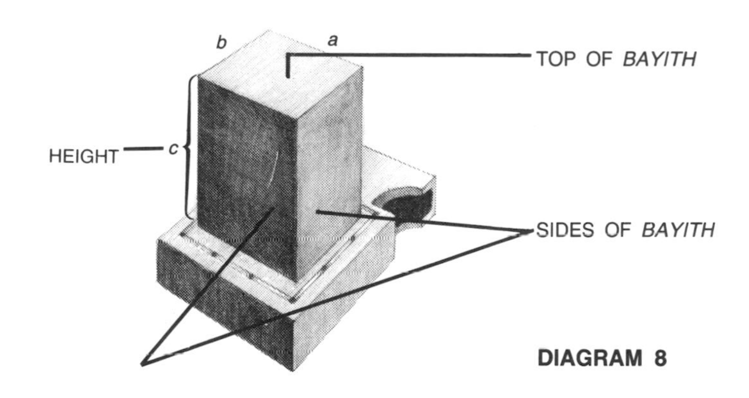

DIAGRAM 8

other words, the *bayith* does not have to be a perfect cube. Since even a slight nick in the sides of the *bayith* may destroy its square shape and make the tefillin *posul*, protective cases are used to store the tefillin. Also, when being worn on the arm under the shirt sleeve, the *shel yad* has another lighter, protective cover, called a *yidel*, which should be removed before reciting the beracha להניח תפילין, and replaced after saying *baruch shem kavod.*[44a] One should slide these coverings on and off very slowly and carefully so that the tefillin do not become damaged.

What in nature is perfectly square? Look around outside. Look around in all the science books. Look here and there, look high and low. Now look again at the tefillin. Amazing! How beautiful! Although it is humanly impossible to make them absolutely square, one thing is certain: they did not fall down from heaven this way.[45] Man, the Jew, made them as perfectly as possible in order to do the will of his Creator.

Both tefillin and their straps are required to be painted black. The black of the straps, however, is a *halacha l'Moshe m'Sinai* while the black of the *bayith* is, according to some authorities, not a Mosaic law.[46] A practical difference occurs when even though black paint chips off the *bayith*, it is still usable when there is no other pair to replace it.

What makes black special from all other colors? Mix any two colors together, and you will always get a third color. Blue with yellow becomes green; green and red become brown; blue and red become purple. Black, however, will not change into any other color in the blending machine. It remains unaffected and unchanged. This special characteristic of tefillin's color hints to the nature of HaShem, for HaShem is unchangeable, as it says, "For I am the L-rd, I do not change" (*Malachi* 3:6).[47]

Why can we not make a pair of tefillin out of cardboard or plastic? They certainly would cost a lot less. The Torah says, "And it [tefillin] shall be for a sign to you upon your hand...that the L-rd's Torah may be in your mouth" (*Shemoth* 13:9). *Chazal* explain that it is permitted to make the tefillin only with what is generally permitted for you to eat – "in your mouth."[48] And it is *halacha l'Moshe m'Sinai* that the material be from the hide of a kosher animal and not from animal bone, or from fish or fowl. However, even though an animal may be prohibited from being eaten because it is a *n'velah* or *t'refeh*, it is still permitted to use its hide to make tefillin.

Since tefillin are made from natural skin and not from wood or plastic, they become part of our body and are not just an artificial badge of honor attached to us. Of course, we have to rise to the occasion by realizing what we are putting on every morning. Perhaps, we should remember that Hashem, as it were, also puts on tefillin every day.[49] Our tefillin describe our relationship with Hashem. Hashem's tefillin describe His relationship with us; for example, one of the inscriptions says, "Who is like Your People Yisroel, one Nation on the earth."[50] We know that Hashem follows His part, but do we fulfill our responsibility?

30 THE TEFILLIN HANDBOOK

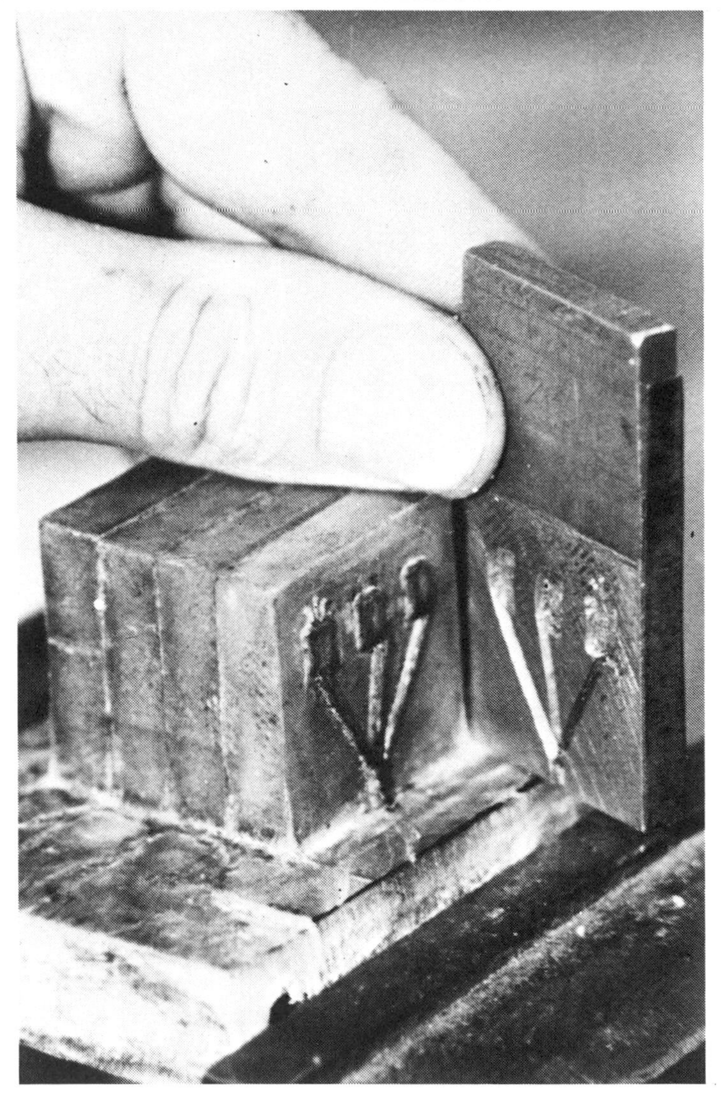

A metal *shin*-mold used in *gassoth* tefillin.

[7] WHY DOES THE *SHEL YAD* HAVE ONE COMPARTMENT FOR ALL THE *PARSHIYOTH* WHILE THE *SHEL ROSH* HAS FOUR SEPARATE COMPARTMENTS?

The *shel yad* is described by the Torah simply as "a sign upon your hand." *Chazal* note that since the word "sign" is written in the singular and not in the plural, only a single *bayith* is called for.[51] Further, in the same way that it is one sign (one *bayith*) on the outside, so also is it one sign (all written on one long parchment) on the inside.

The *shel rosh* is called *totofoth*, frontlets. In the four *parshiyoth* of tefillin the word *totofoth* appears three times. Rabbi Yishmael says that two of the three times it is written *totofath* טטפת (singular) and once *totofoth* טוטפות (plural).[52] Since the smallest number of any plural is two, he calculated that two (*totofoth*) plus one and one (*totofath*) equal four; therefore, we have four separate compartments.

Rabbi Akiva learns this idea directly from the word *totofoth* [טוטפות], which is a combination of two foreign words, *tat* [טוט] in the Coptic language and *foth* [פות] in the African language. Each word means the number "two," and together they add up to four, indicating the four compartments in the tefillin *shel rosh*.

Adding together these four with the one compartment of the *shel yad*, one has five – symbolic of the five senses.[53] Since the hands are mostly associated with the sense of touch, the *shel yad* represents using this sense and all other actions of the body *l'shem shemayim*. The other four sense organs – the eyes, ears, palate and nose – are located in the head. Consequently, the four compartments of the *shel rosh* indicate the dedication of these four senses to the service of their Creator.

[8] WHY IS THE *SHEL YAD* PUT ON FIRST AND THE *SHEL ROSH* TAKEN OFF FIRST?

The Torah tells us, "You shall bind them [tefillin] for a sign upon your hand and they shall be for frontlets between your eyes" (*Devorim* 6:8). From here we see that the binding on the hand (*shel yad*) is first since it is mentioned first.[54] "They shall be" tells us that as long as the *shel rosh* is between your eyes, "they" both the *shel rosh* and the *shel yad* should be worn. Therefore, we take the *shel rosh* off first so that at no time will the *shel rosh* be worn alone without the *shel yad*.

To assist in following these rules, be sure to take out first the *shel yad* from your tefillin bag and put it on before taking out the *shel rosh*.[55] Only after you have made the beracha and wound the strap down to the wrist, do you then take out the *shel rosh* and put it on your head (see Appendix I, Practical Guide: How to Put on Tefillin, p. 55).

Before taking off the *shel rosh* untie the three windings around the middle finger. The *shel rosh* should be removed with the left hand (weaker hand) to show a reluctance in taking it off.[56] (A left-handed person would use his weaker, right hand.)[57]

Since one has to put on the *shel yad* first, it should always be placed on the same side of the bag so that one will always take it out first. Some have the *minhag* of wrapping the straps differently around the *shel rosh* and the *shel yad*. These reminders are necessary so that we do not mistakenly take out the *shel rosh* first.[58] Even so, if a person accidentally touched or took out the *shel rosh* first, he should *not* put it on. Instead, he should put it back and take out the *shel yad*.[59]

Because of the love for the mitzvah, it is the *minhag* to kiss the tefillin when taking them out and putting them back into their bag.[60]

Be sure not to hang or carry the tefillin by the straps.[61] Even when the tefillin are inside the bag, care should be taken not to carry the bag by the corner with the fingers lest they fall to the ground, *chas v'shalom*. Instead, they should be carried securely underneath the bag or firmly held by the hand against the chest.

When a person leaves his home for an overnight trip, he should take along his tefillin so that he will have them to wear the next morning.[62]

In the year 1490, Rabbi Yosef Gikatilya, the author of *Shaarei Orah*, became seriously ill and was on the verge of death. Suddenly, he saw before him two men weighing his sins against his merits. When he saw that they equalled one another, he immediately asked that his tefillin be brought to him. As soon as he put them on, he started to feel better and, not long thereafter, fully regained his health.

Various stages in the making of the *shel rosh* in *gassoth* tefillin.

Various stages in the making of the *shel yad*.

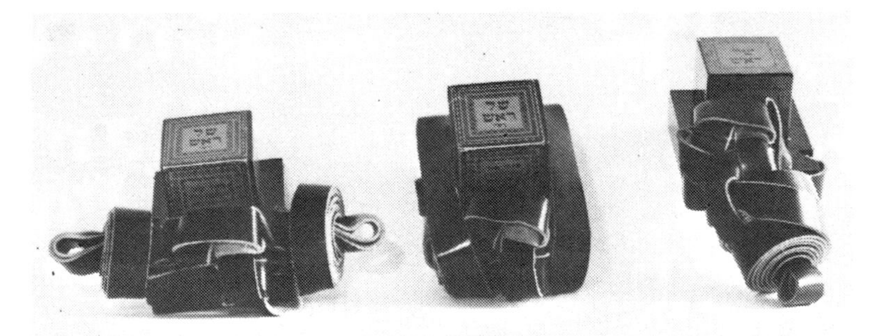

Kanfe yona: various ways of winding the straps around the *bayith* to resemble the wings of a dove. The middle one is the most common way. (Note that the knot is placed on top instead of underneath the *bayith*.)

[9] HOW MANY BERACHOTH ARE MADE? MUST ONE STAND WHEN PUTTING ON TEFILLIN?

The number of *berachoth* which are made on tefillin is a complicated question dating from the time of the *Gemora* and depends today on *minhag*.[63] Most say two *berachoth*, "...*lahaw-niach tefillin* [לְהָנִיחַ תְּפִילִין] on the *shel yad* and "...*al mitzvath tefillin*" [עַל מִצְוַת תְּפִילִין] on the *shel rosh*. Others say only the first beracha – the custom common among Sephardim and some Chassidic communities.

Special care must be taken not to talk between putting on the *shel yad* and the *shel rosh*.[64] This rule applies no matter if one or two *berachoth* are recited. Pretend that you are swimming under water; would you dare try to breathe in air at a time like that? Indeed, one should not even answer *kaddish* or *kedusha*; instead, one must stop and listen. We can understand how important this law is when we realize that, in the times of old, a Jewish soldier who failed to keep silent when putting on his tefillin was sent home from the battle front – a sign of grave disgrace.[65]

If one who normally says two *berachoth* did speak before putting on the *shel rosh*, then:

[1] if he answered *amen, kaddish* or *kedusha*, he need only say עַל מִצְוַת on the *shel rosh*;[66]

[2] if he said anything else, then he should recite two *berachoth* on the *shel rosh* – first עַל מִצְוַת, then (after the *shel rosh* is in place) לְהָנִיחַ on the *shel yad*, being sure to

move the *shel yad* slightly.[67] Afterwards, *baruch shem kavod* is said.

Those, however, who normally make one beracha, need to say only עַל מִצְוַת תְּפִילִין on the *shel rosh*.[68]

One should be careful to say *lahawniach* לְהָנִיחַ tefillin, and not *lahahniach* לְהַנִיחַ tefillin. What a world of difference one vowel sound can make! Instead of saying "...for the placing [לְהָנִיחַ *lahawniach*] of tefillin," one could wrongly say "...for the leaving off [לְהַנִיחַ *lahahniach*] of tefillin."[69] The first one is spelled with a *kametz* and the second one with a *pasach*. Also, when saying עַל מִצְוַת *al mitzvath tefillin*, be careful not to say עַל מִצְוֹת *al mitzvoth tefillin* since the *shel rosh* is only one mitzvah and not two mitzvoth.

Did you ever wonder why we say *lahawniach* [לְהָנִיחַ] tefillin and not *likshor* [לִקְשׁוֹר] tefillin, which would be more like the *nusach* of the *posuk*, וקשרתם לאות על ידך? One commentator points out that originally the mitzvah was to wear tefillin all day long.[70] Had *likshor*, to bind, been used, we might have thought that the mitzvah was fulfilled simply by wearing them for an instant. לְהָנִיחַ, on the other hand, implies placing them on for a longer period of time.

For those who say two berachoth, the second beracha is said only after the *shel rosh* is placed on the head. When saying the beracha one should be sure that his yarmulke is on his head. Now, one should carefully press down the straps tightly around one's whole head, making certain that:

[1] the black of the straps is showing;

[2] the *bayith* is centered on the hair-line, "between the eyes" (see Diagrams 4 and 5);

[3] the knot is centered in the back of the head (see Diagram 9).

Then, only *after* one is certain that his tefillin and straps are adjusted, should he say "*baruch shem kavod malchutho l'olam va'ed.*[71]

Many ask: why do we say *baruch shem kavod* after saying the beracha *al mitzvath tefillin* on the *shel rosh*? If a person makes a mistaken beracha, he says *baruch shem kavod*. But, here in tefillin, the second beracha is required for Ashkenazim. So why do we say *baruch shem kavod*?

The *Mishna Berura* explains that the second beracha is necessary, but we say *baruch shem kavod* only as an extraordinary measure to remove all shadow of doubt [לרווחא דמלתא] since there are some authorities who do not require the second beracha.[72]

Many people mention the names of the four *parshiyoth* as part of the *tefillah* (*l'shem yechud*) which is recited before laying tefillin. Indeed, it is important to say this prayer since it can increase one's *kavannah*, and *Chazal* have taught us that the mitzvah of serving HaShem "with all your heart" (*Devorim* 11:13) includes preparing your *kavannah* before you do a mitzvah.[73]

If a person has to go to the bathroom during *davening* , he should remove his tefillin and, when he returns, he should put them on with a beracha.[74]

38 THE TEFILLIN HANDBOOK

The knot should be centered on the back of the head at the base of the skull but still on the bone. Not too high and not too low, not to the right and not to the left (see Diagram 9).

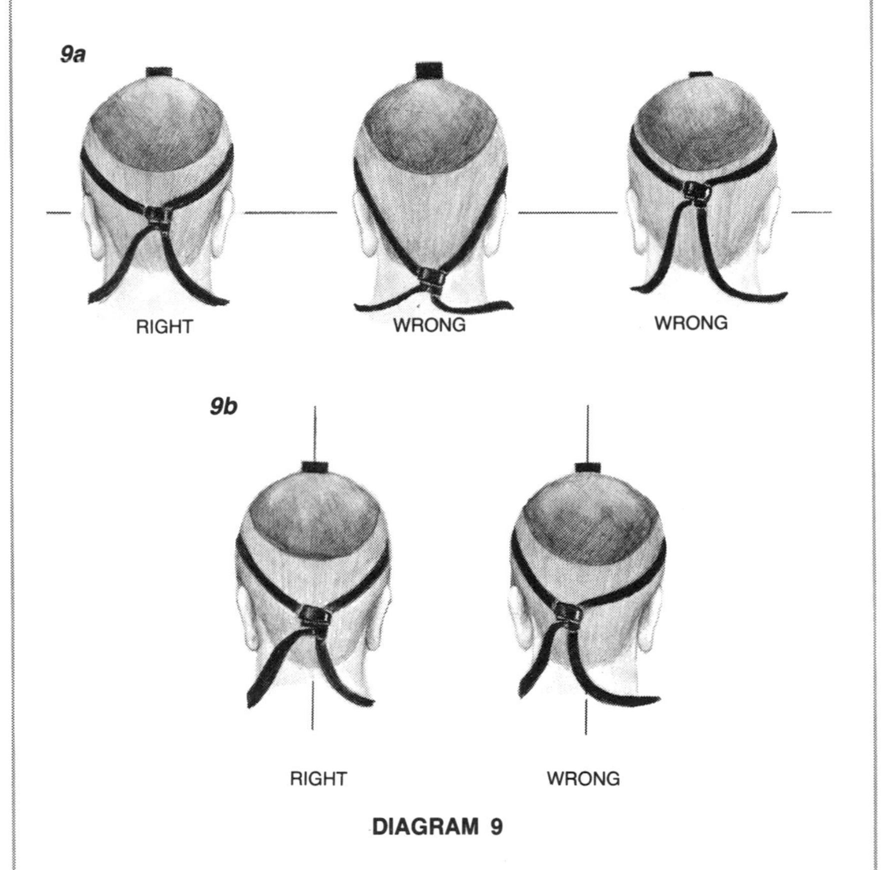

DIAGRAM 9

These exact positions have symbolic meaning. On the bone in the back of the head and not in the hollow of the neck points out that Israel should be on top and not on the bottom (see

Diagram 9a). Directly opposite the front of the face and not on the sides hints that Israel should be in front and not in back (see Diagram 9b). The Maharsha explains that the crown of Torah mentioned in *Pirke Avoth* (4:17) applies to the tefillin *shel rosh*.[76] Therefore, "being on top" indicates that the Jewish People will be supreme through Torah; and "being in front" refers to a Jew with the crown of Torah coming before the crowns of *Kehunah* and *Malchuth*.

The *minhag* among most communities is to stand when putting on tefillin and when taking them off. The Sephardic community is a major exception since its custom is to sit while putting on the *shel yad*.[77]

[10] ARE STRAPS OF THE TEFILLIN ABSOLUTELY NECESSARY? MUST THEY ALSO BE BLACK? HOW MANY TIMES IS THE STRAP WOUND AROUND THE ARM? THE PERMANENT KNOTS OF THE *SHEL ROSH* AND THE *SHEL YAD* LOOK LIKE WHICH HEBREW LETTERS?

A kite without a string is still a kite, but tefillin without their straps are not kosher tefillin. Why?

Since the Torah tells us to *bind* on ourselves the tefillin, we understand that by simply balancing one on the head and pressing the other against the arm we are not fulfilling the mitzvah of binding. Therefore, straps – called *retzuoth* – are an essential part of the mitzvah and are one of the eight laws of tefillin listed by the Rambam as *halacha l'Moshe m'Sinai.*[78]

Still, "binding" implies making a knot to tie something securely. But the knots of the *shel yad* and *shel rosh* are permanent, and all that we do is tighten the straps on our arm and head. *Chazal* have explained, however, that this tightening is all that is necessary to fulfill the words of the Torah, "to bind them."[79]

The *retzuoth* are made from the hide of a kosher animal. If this seems obvious to you by now, then listen to this true story from the time of Rabbi Akiva.[80] Once, one of Rabbi Akiva's students came into the *Beth HaMidrash* wearing tefillin with straps made of blueish wool which was obviously against the *halacha*. The student, however, must have been unaware of this law. Rabbi Akiva did not say anything to him. His fellow *chachamim* wondered how such a *tzaddik* like Rabbi Akiva could allow this mistake. But then they realized that he, in fact, had not seen the student, for had he seen him, Rabbi Akiva surely would have told him the proper *halacha*. We see from this story, interestingly, that under normal circumstances the teacher is held responsible for his student's shortcomings and mistakes.

It is *halacha l'Moshe m'Sinai* that the *retzuoth* must be colored black on the outside. The *Mishna Berura* warns us that if the black paint fades or chips off, it must be repainted.[81] Not any black paint will do; so do not go down into your father's workshop looking for any regular black paint. Instead, show the tefillin to a rabbi or take them directly to a tefillin-maker to touch them up.

Further, painting the straps black, like many other steps in the making of tefillin, must be done specifically for the purpose of fulfilling the mitzvah of tefillin, לִשְׁמָה. Make sure that the place where the *shel yad* is tightened is completely black since pulling the strap makes it likely that the paint will wear off. The width of the *retzuah* is the length of a barley grain, which according to the Chazon Ish is eleven millimeters (slightly under half an inch) and according to Rabbi A.C. Na'eh is ten millimeters (.39 inch).[82]

When wearing tefillin, one should be very careful that only the black side of the strap shows. This rule applies (1) along the circumference of the head and (2) along the first complete turn turn of the *retzuah* closest to the *bayith* on th *shel yad.*[83] Of course, it is best to have the whole length of the *retzuoth* showing on the black side.

The right strap of the *shel rosh* should extend at least until the waist while the minimum length of the left strap is down to the chest.[84] The custom today is to have both straps extend at least to the navel (*tabor*). This hints to how far the influence of the mitzvoth affect this world – until the very core (*tabor*, i.e., center of the earth); and not like some who say that HaShem's influence only reaches down to the moon (i.e., celestial influences).[85]

When putting on the *shel yad*, most people wind the *retzuah* seven times on the arm from the elbow to the wrist. They stop at the wrist because many *poskim* hold that the mitzvah of the *shel yad* does not extend beyond this point. Then they put on the *shel rosh* and, afterwards, return to wind the *retzuah* of the *shel yad* three times around the middle finger (see Diagram 10).

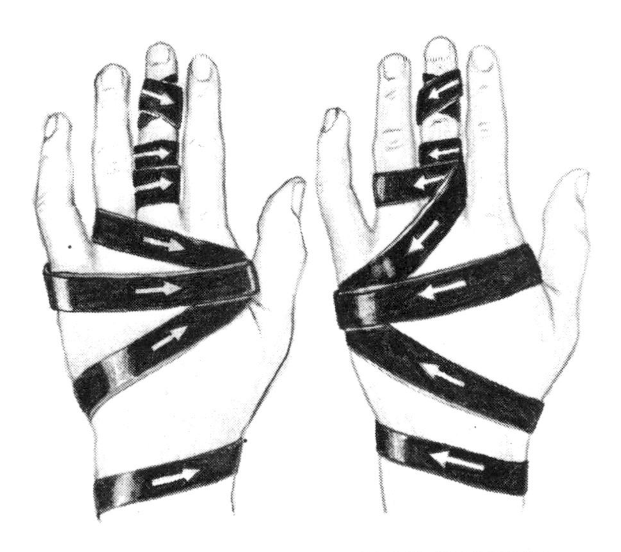

ASHKENAZ VERSION SEPHARDI VERSION

DIAGRAM 10

The knot of the *shel rosh* is shaped into the letter *dalet* [ד] and the knot of the *shel yad*, into the letter *yud* [י] (see photographs, p.49). Although some have the *minhag* of making two *dalets* for the *shel rosh* one inside the other, the *Mishna Berura* suggests that one *dalet* is preferable.[86] Since the *yud*-knot of the *shel yad* should be tight against the *bayith*, a sinew thread is sometimes used to hold it against the *bayith*.[87]

[11] WHAT ARE THE *TITURA* AND THE *MA'ABARTA*?

The *titura*, an Aramaic word meaning "bridge," is the name given to the base of the tefillin, and like the *bayith*, is made of leather and painted black. The mitzvah *min hamuvchar* is to have the *bayith, titura* and *ma'abarta* all made together from a single piece of leather.[88]

Extending from the *titura* is the *ma'abarta*, which has this name because the strap passes (*ma'abar*) through it (see Diagram 11). It is considered separate from the *titura* since the

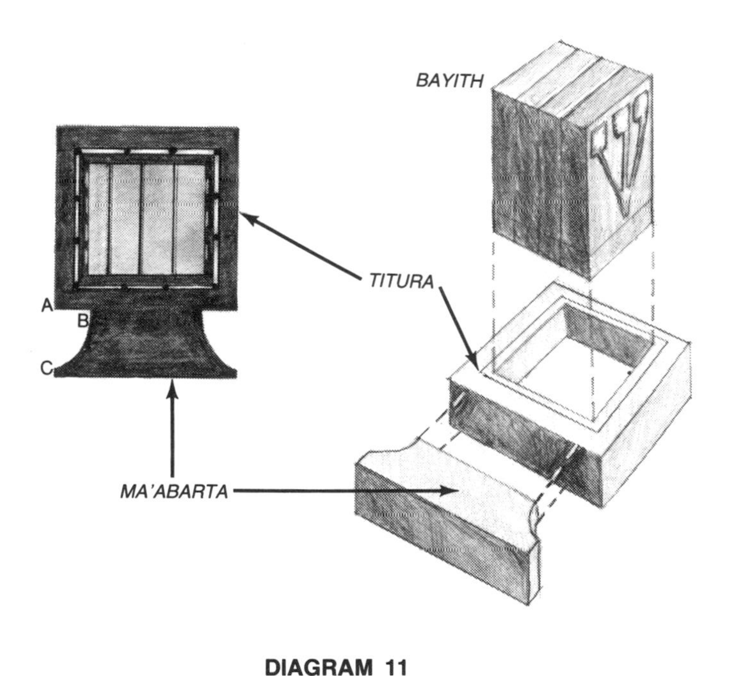

DIAGRAM 11

titura is required to be perfectly square. Therefore, from the edge of the *titura* to the back of the *ma'abarta*, the leather is cut out in the shape of a semi-circle (see points A–B–C) to show that it is not part of the *titura*.

Both the *titura* and the *ma'abarta* are *halacha l'Moshe m'Sinai*, and tefillin without them are not considered kosher.[89]

In *dakoth* and *peshutim* tefillin, a square hole is cut in the upper "tongue" of the *titura*, and a separately made *bayith* with flaps is squeezed through the hole, the flaps remaining between the upper and lower "tongues" of the *titura* (see Diagram 12).

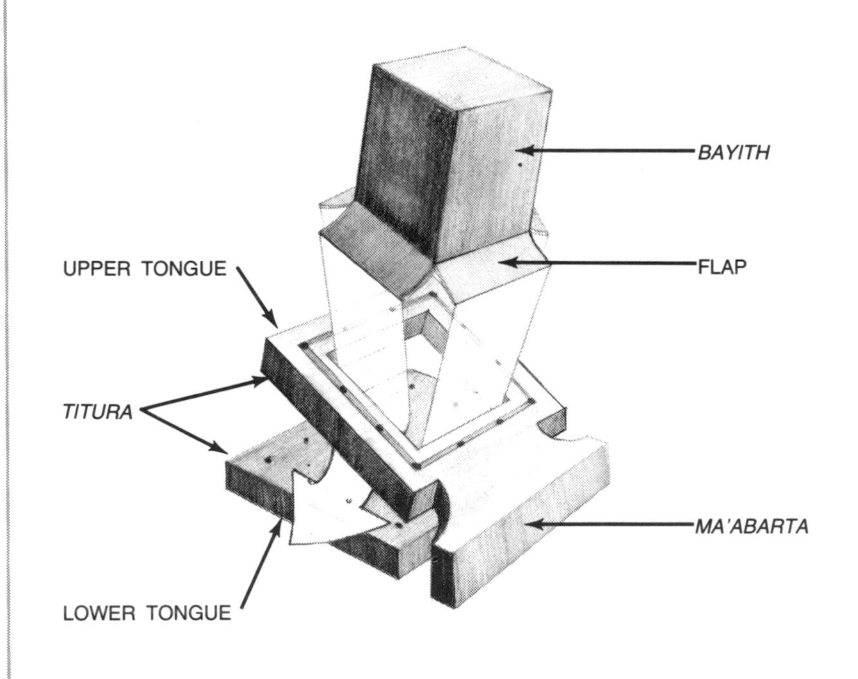

DIAGRAM 12

Next, the *titura* is closed tight and sewn together with a sinew thread, special care being taken that the thread goes through the flaps of the *bayith* as well (see also photographs p. 34, showing stages in the making of *gassoth* tefillin).

Just as the *batim* must be made by an expert tefillin-maker, so the *parshiyoth* must be written by a reliable *sofer*. The laws of writing *S'TaM* are very intricate and numerous, and even a slight mistake in one letter can invalidate the whole *parsha*. Therefore, when purchasing tefillin, one should investigate the *kashruth* of both the *batim* and the *parshiyoth*.[89a]

In all types of tefillin, before the *titura* is sewn together the *parshiyoth* are rolled up and tied with calf's hair, covered with a piece of parchment (*matlith*) and then tied again. And as we see from the following story, sometimes even more can go into the *titura*:

Zev, son of the Admor Rebbe Michel of Zalotshov, was not distinguished in his youth by his scholarship or outstanding character. A few months before his Bar Mitzvah, his father asked the *sofer* to bring him the *parshiyoth* before placing them in the tefillin. When the *sofer* brought them, Rebbe Michel took the *bayith*, turned it upside down and opened up the "tongues" of the *titura* in order to look inside. Suddenly, with tremendous emotion, he broke into tears and just kept crying and crying. The tears rolled down his cheeks and into the *bayith*. Only after it was filled with tears did the Admor stop crying. He emptied the tears and let the tefillin dry out thoroughly. Then, he carefully put the *parshiyoth* into the tefillin and told the *sofer* to have the "tongues" sewn together.

On the day of his Bar Mitzvah, the Admor's son Zev put on the tefillin for the first time. Immediately, he felt the spirit of HaShem enter him and change him and, right then and there, vowed to dedicate his life to the service of HaShem and his fellow man.

[12] CAN TEFILLIN BE WORN AT NIGHT? WHY ARE THEY NOT WORN ON SHABBAT AND YOM TOV? WHEN ARE TEFILLIN FIRST WORN?

According to most authorities, any time, day or night, weekday, Shabbat and Yom Tov, the Torah permits the wearing of tefillin. Why, then, do we not wear them at night or on Shabbat and Yom Tov? *Chazal* have answered this question in detail.[90]

Sleeping with tefillin on is forbidden since we cannot control our passing gas, which is forbidden when wearing tefillin. Since the onset of darkness is the beginning of sleep-time, the *Rabbonim* forbade wearing tefillin at nighttime.

One commentator cites a scriptural allusion to help us understand why passing gas is not permitted.[91] It says in *Tehillim* (49:21), "A man who is in honor and understands not is like the beasts that perish." *Chazal* call tefillin "honor" as it says in *Esther* (8:16), "The Jews had light, and gladness, and joy, and honor." "Honor," says the *Gemora* in *Megilla* 16b, refers to tefillin. Passing gas is the animal part of us and is not proper while wearing tefillin. Now we can re-read the *posuk* in *Tehillim*: "A man who is in honor because he is wearing tefillin and does not understand the law about not passing gas is like the non-understanding beasts that perish."

When is nighttime for the purposes of this prohibition? If the sun has just set and we have not yet laid tefillin, we are still permitted to put them on, but without a beracha.[92] However, after the stars have come out, we are no longer able to put them on.

Before dawn is also considered nighttime. At a certain period after dawn, when "one can recognize a casual friend at a distance of four *amoth*," even though the sky is barely light, we may put on tefillin and make the *berachoth*.[93] During the winter when the sun rises late, it is permitted to put on tefillin before dawn provided that it is impossible to do so later. However, one should say the *berachoth* only after dawn, also moving the tefillin slightly. If a beracha was mistakenly made while it was still night, a second beracha is not necessary.[94]

There are two reasons which *Chazal* give for not wearing tefillin on Shabbat and Yom Tov. Just as two witnesses are needed to establish a fact in Jewish courts, a Jew needs two signs or witnesses to show that he is truly living his Jewishness. On weekdays, the two witnesses are tefillin ("it shall be for you as a sign") and *brith milah* ("the sign of the holy covenant"). Shabbat and Yom Tov are also called signs, as it says, "between Me and the Children of Israel, it [Shabbat] shall be an eternal sign.''[95] Therefore, tefillin are not necessary on these days since the sign of Shabbat and Yom Tov replaces the sign of tefillin.

One could ask what is wrong with having all three signs together. And the answer is that the sign of tefillin would be cheapened (זלזול לאות) by the already existing sign of Shabbat.[96] In addition, tefillin are forbidden on Shabbat because one might accidentally go outside with them on and be guilty of moving an object from one domain to another.[97]

We can also give a third answer from a different approach. Tefillin are one of the signs of a Jew. They are a daily reminder of our obligations and special closeness to HaShem. As one of the first mitzvoth of the day, tefillin can have an effect on us for the whole day. Shabbat and Yom Tov are also reminders of our obligations and closeness to HaShem. Special *davening* and the Torah reading in shul, festive meals, singing *zemiroth* around the table are all strong, visible signs of being a Jew. Therefore, on these days we do not need the sign of tefillin to remind us of our Yiddishkeit.

On *Chol HaMoed*, the *minhag* in *Eretz Yisroel* is not to wear tefillin, even privately. In *Chutz L'aretz*, however, many follow the Rama's halachic decision and wear tefillin.[98]

Tefillin are required to be worn at age thirteen, but various *minhagim* determine how long before age thirteen the young man practices wearing tefillin. Most begin about a month or two before the Bar Mitzvah while some wait until the Bar Mitzvah day

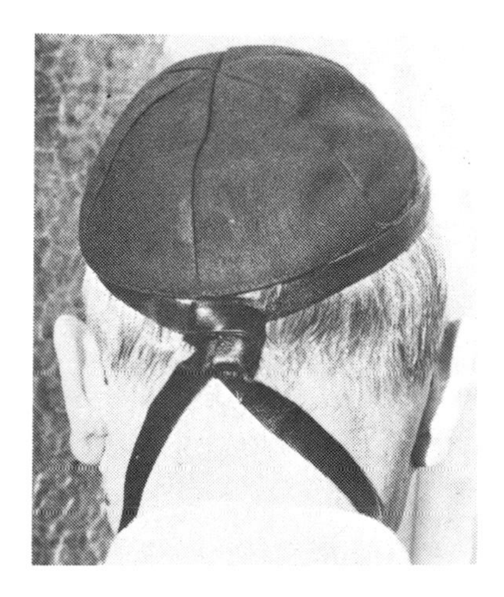

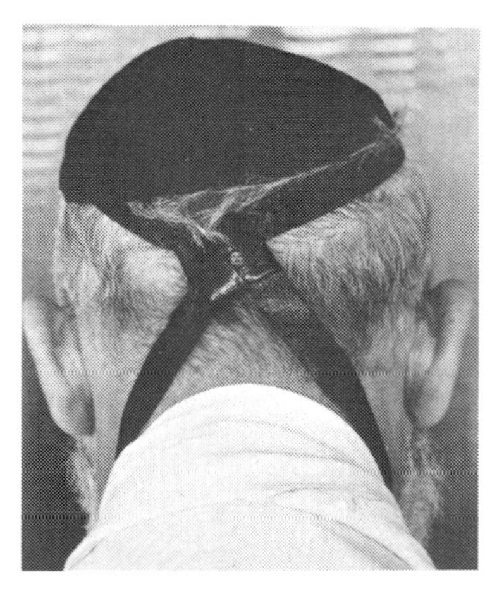

The *dalet*-knot of the *shel rosh*. Left: single *dalet*; right: double *dalet*.

Close-up of single *dalet*-knot (left) and *yud*-knot (right).

itself.[99] Moroccan Jews are unique; they start a year before the Bar Mitzvah!

Why are there such differences in *minhagim*? And why is there not a mitzvah of *chinuch* by tefillin? Young boys put on *tzitzits* and take the *lulav*, but we do not train them early in tefillin. Why not?

The *Gemora* is *Succah* 42a says that once a child can reliably watch over tefillin, he càn begin wearing them. ''Watching over tefillin'' means not going into the bathroom while wearing them, not sleeping with them on, and not passing air while having them on – the concept of *guf naki* (clean body). Since a child is not able to maintain a *guf naki*, there is no mitzvah of *chinuch*. Only as he approaches his Bar Mitzvah is he considered mature enough to control himself, with different *minhagim* exactly how much before age thirteen.

[13] WHY IS THE LETTER *SHIN* FOUND ONLY ON THE *SHEL ROSH*? HOW MANY TIMES? CAN IT BE SIMPLY PAINTED ON? WHY DOES ONE *SHIN* HAVE FOUR HEADS?

The Hebrew letter *shin* surely must be a very special letter to be found on the tefillin not just once but twice. What makes it so unique a letter that it gets double honor over twenty-one other letters?

The *shin* in tefillin is *halacha l'Moshe m'Sinai* and is made in the leather of the *shel rosh* itself.[100] On the right side of the one wearing tefillin is a three-headed *shin*, and on his left side is a four-headed *shin*. The *shin* should touch the *titura* and is *mihudar* if shaped like the *shin* in the *Sefer Torah*.[101]

It is not kosher halachically simply to paint on a *shin* or to glue on a piece of leather cut out in the shape of a *shin*. Usually a metal stencil-molded type *shin* is placed on the outside and set under pressure until the soft leather bulges out in the form of a *shin*[102] (see photographs, p. 30).

Although there are many reasons why there are two *shins*, why one has four heads and why they are on the *shel rosh*, we will offer just a few.

The two *shins* hint to the 613 mitzvoth.[103] How? The *gematria* of each *shin* is 300, and two *shins* make 600. The two *shins* spell the word *shesh* [שֵׁשׁ] six, giving us 606. The number of heads on each *shin* is three and four, which together are seven. 606 plus seven is 613, indicating the *Taryag mitzvoth*.

The four-headed *shin* hints to the script used in the original Tablets from *Har Sinai*.[104] The letters of the Tablets were bored all the way through the stone. Therefore, the *shin* used on the Tablets had three hollowed-space heads, but for us to allude to this *shin*, we make four heads because that leaves three spaces in between – like the way that it was found in the Tablets (see Diagram 13).

Why are the *shins* on the *shel rosh*? When we recall the *posuk*, "And all the peoples of the earth shall see that the name of the L-rd is called upon you; and they shall be afraid of you" (*Devorim* 28:10), and how *Chazal* tell us that this refers to the

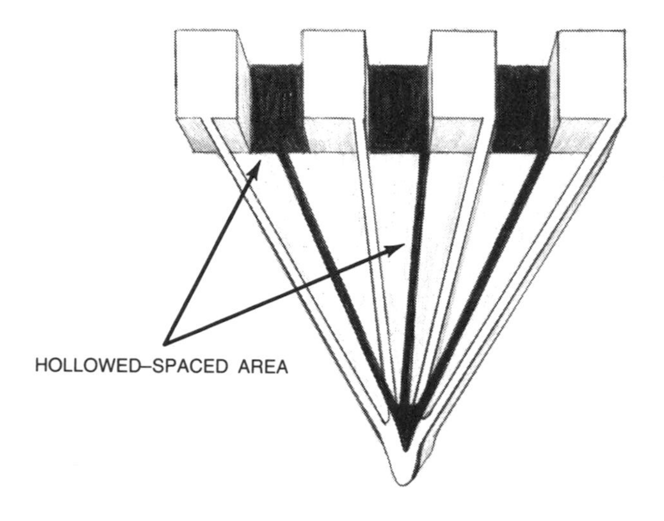

DIAGRAM 13

tefillin *shel rosh*, an obvious question arises. How in fact does the *posuk* teach us of the *shel rosh*?

Listen carefully to the answer. The four letter Name of HaShem in *aat-bash** spells *matz-patz* [מצפ"צ].[105] The *gematria* of these four letters is 40, 90, 80, and 90, which add up to 300. Therefore, the letter *shin* on the *shel rosh* which all the world can see will cause every one to be in awe since the *shin* (300) hints to the name of HaShem.

---

* *aat-bash* is a method of interchanging letters. The first letter of the Hebrew alphabet is replaced by the last letter , *alef* for *toph* (*aa't* א–ת), the second with the next to last, *beth* for *shin* (*ba'sh* ב–ש), and so on.

Why is the four-headed *shin* on the left side of the one who is wearing tefillin? Actually, this *shin* is on the right side of anyone facing the wearer of tefillin. One commentator explains that HaShem is the one who is facing us, as it says in *Tehillim* 16:8, "I have set the L-rd always before me."[106] Therefore, the four-headed *shin* of the Tablets is on His right side, the side which represents special holiness, as it says, "from His right hand went a fiery law for them" (*Devorim* 33:2).

The two *shins* spell the word *saas* [שָׂשׂ], joy.[107] The mitzvah of tefillin is a joy and an honor. To show us how high tefillin can bring a person who understands what he is really wearing, *Chazal* tell us the following story:[108] Once when Abaye was together with Rabba, he noticed Rabba in an exhilarated state of great joy. Abaye cautioned him: "Should we not be careful lest we become overjoyous and light-headed, as it says, '...and rejoice with trembling' (*Tehillim* 2:II)?" Rabba turned to him with a gentle smile and replied: "I just put on my tefillin which are a witness that I have my Master's task before me to do. Although I am rejoicing because I am wearing Tefillin, the tefillin are also safeguarding me from becoming light-headed."

Tefillin are a precious gift from HaShem to each and every one of us. The very name of *Sha–Kai*, *shin–dalet–yud* is spelled out on us every time we put them on.[109] So let us involve ourselves in seriously studying the laws of tefillin and in understanding their meaning and holiness. For then we can use each morning of our lives to feel closer to HaShem and, thereby, give the whole day greater joy and purpose. Tefillin are a firm ladder upon which we can climb up and up in our service of the Almighty.[110] Now it is up to us to work hard and strive to achieve their potential. *B'hatzlacha*!

A tefillin-maker at work.

APPENDIX I

Practical Guide: How to put on Tefillin

Note: Numbers in brackets refer the reader back to "Answers with Explanations."

1. Take out the tefillin *shel yad* first, leaving the *shel rosh* in the bag and unravel the strap [8]. It is necessary to have in mind the purposes tefillin, which are to proclaim the unity of HaShem and to remember His taking us out of Egypt. Therefore, many are accustomed to say the *l'shem yechud* before putting on the *shel yad* [9]. It is customary, as well, to kiss the tefillin now when taking them out and later when putting them back [8].
2. While still standing (except for Sephardim), a right-handed person should place the *shel yad* on the middle of the biceps muscle of his left arm, slightly tilting the *bayith* towards the heart. A left-handed person should place it on his right arm [4]. Some take off the protective cardboard cover until after saying *baruch shem kavod* [6].
3. Before actually tightening the strap, one should carefully

and thoughtfully say the beracha of ...*lahawniach* לְהָנִיחַ tefillin [9].

4. Without speaking, one tightens the strap at the *bayith*, being careful that the black side is showing and nothing (e.g., shirt sleeve) is under the *bayith*. Then one winds it seven times down to the wrist and temporarily ties the rest around the palm of his hand [10]. The shirt sleeve may be pulled down over the *bayith* at this time.
5. Next, while remaining absolutely silent, one takes the *shel rosh* out of the bag and places it on his head. Some have the *minhag* of first looking at the two *shins* and kissing the knot. If he follows the custom of making two *berachoth*, he now says "...*al mitzvath* עַל מִצְוַת tefillin" and only then centers and tightens it down on his head, being careful both to center the knot of the *shel rosh* and to keep the black side of the straps showing. (Remember that the knot should be on the bone at the back of the head just above the hollow leading to the neck.) Immediately thereafter, one says *baruch shem kavod malchutho l'olam va'ed* [5,9,10]. Then one makes sure that the two straps come down in front of his body.
6. Now one unwraps the strap around his palm and winds it three times around the middle finger while reciting the *posukim* in Hoshea (2:21-22), "And I will betroth you to Me for ever..." [10]. (See Diagram 10 for several ways to wrap the middle finger.)
7. One should touch the tefillin regularly, especially when

reciting the *Kiriyath Shema*, "and you shall bind them as a sign on your hand, and they shall be as frontlets between your eyes" [5].

8. After the *davening* is completed, before removing the *shel rosh*, one should stand up and unwind the strap from around the fingers and wind this part again around his palm. Using his weaker hand, one should carefully remove the *shel rosh*, enclose it in its special case, wrap up the straps on each side, and return it to the bag [8]. As mentioned, it is customary to kiss the tefillin.
9. Then one unwinds the strap from his palm and arm, loosening the bond at the *bayith* in order to remove the *shel yad*.
10. Finally, one encloses the *shel yad* in its case, wraps the strap around and returns it to the bag, being sure always to place it on one particular side. In this way, the next time one puts on tefillin, he will know exactly which side to reach for the *shel yad* first without touching the *shel rosh* [8].

APPENDIX II

Practical Guide: What happens if...?

TAKING OUT THE TEFILLIN

1. If one starts to take the *shel rosh* instead of the *shel yad*, even inside the bag:

   Leave go of the *shel rosh* and proceed to take out the *shel yad*.

2. If, *chas v'shalom*, they should drop on the floor with their protective cases:

   The *minhag* is to give charity instead of fasting. Obviously, they should be picked up right away and kissed. Check to make sure that they were not damaged, especially the top corners of the *bayith*.

3. If both are taken out by mistake:

   Return the *shel rosh* into the bag.

SHEL YAD

1. If one forgot to say the beracha until after he finished winding the strap down to the wrist:

   Say the beracha and then move the *bayith* slightly back and forth.

2. If one realized, after making the beracha, that the *bayith* was

not in the proper position (for instance, it was too close to the elbow or it was facing out instead of toward the heart):

He should adjust it now – it is still part of the mitzvah of *shel yad* – without speaking. The beracha is not repeated.

3. If the *yud*-knot is not firmly against the *bayith*:

   See p. 42.

4. When a left-handed person borrows a pair of tefillin from someone who is right-handed (or vice versa), should he change the knot?

   No. It is sufficient to turn the *bayith* upside-down (i.e., with the *ma'abarta* towards the hand).

5. If one has a watch on his wrist:

   One is not required to remove it although the custom is to do so.

THE BERACHA

1. Just when one is about to make the beracha להניח, and everything is in place, the *chazan* starts *kaddish*:

   Wait and do not say the beracha until after he has finished *kaddish*. Obviously, one should answer *kaddish*.

2. When saying the beracha להניח, one forgot to say "who has sanctified us by His mitzvoth and commanded us..."; that is, one said, ברוך אתה ה׳ אלקינו מלך העולם – להניח תפילין:

   One is not יוצא and must repeat the beracha.

3. By mistake, one says על מצות תפילין on the *shel yad* instead of להניח תפילין:

   If one's *minhag* is to say one beracha, then one need not do anything; he is יצא.

   If one's *minhag* is to say two berachoth, then:

   (a) if one realizes his mistake right away, before tightening the knot, he should say the proper beracha immediately.

   (b) after tightening the knot, however, some authorities hold that one should say להניח on the *shel rosh* while other authorities hold that no beracha is necessary on the *shel rosh. L'halacha*, one should say להניח.

BETWEEN *SHEL YAD* AND *SHEL ROSH*

1. Before putting on the *shel rosh*, someone accidentally spoke – even one word:

   Put on the *shel rosh* and say על מצות (this applies even to those people whose *minhag* is not to say a beracha on the *shel rosh*), and then after the *shel rosh* is in place, those who say two berachoth should say להניח on the *shel yad*, moving the *bayith* slightly back and forth.

2. Should one answer *kaddish, kedusha* and *amen* before putting on the *shel rosh*?

   See p. 35.

3. Can one motion to someone else, point to something, or signal in any way in response to someone else?

It is better not to unless it is directly connected with the mitzvah of tefillin. There should be as short a time-lapse as possible between the *shel yad* and the *shel rosh*.

4. One has to go to the bathroom:

   Take off the *shel yad* and cover it. After returning, put it on again with a beracha. (See "Notes" 74, for dis– cussion of how various situations alter the *halacha*.)

SHEL ROSH

1. *Kaddish* is begun just as one is about to put on the *shel rosh*. Should one wait or should one finish putting it on as fast as possible (i.e., say the beracha – if it is one's *minhag* – *and move the bayith* to the middle of the hairline) so that one can answer *kaddish*?

   Yes, if one is sure not to forget all these essential steps.

2. After the beracha was said, the *bayith* was not moved back and forth and centered (because it had already been centered before making the beracha):

   According to most authorities the beracha on the *shel rosh* was לבטלה – a beracha said in vain. Therefore, extreme care should always be taken to say the beracha while the *shel rosh* is approximately centered on the head. After the beracha is said, it should be accurately centered with its knot on the bone in the back of the head, and then the straps around the head should be pressed down firmly. Only then is *baruch shem kavod* said.

3. The unpainted sides of the straps are left showing:

   (a) Along the circumference of the head: it is required to reverse the straps.

   (b) From the knot down: it is not required to do so, but it is better if possible. If "(a)" is not discovered immediately, the *minhag* is to give charity. (This custom also applies to the *shel yad* for the first winding around the arm.)

4. While pressing down the straps around the head, one realizes that the knot lies below its proper place. Which is better: to have the *bayith* extend over the hair-line slightly on the forehead (so that the knot is in its proper place), or to have the knot lower (so that the *bayith* is in its proper place)?

   The knot should be lower, but not so low as to be on the neck where there is no hair. Later the knot should be readjusted.

DURING DAVENING

1. One has to leave to go to the bathroom:

   Take off the tefillin in the same order as normally done. They do not have to be wrapped up in their boxes, but something should be placed over them, such as the tefillin bag. Afterwards, put them on with a beracha. (See Note 74).

2. If one accidently passed gas:

Be sure never to do it again. If one senses that he will continue to pass gas, the tefillin should be removed. When they are put back on, a beracha must be recited.

3. If the strap on the arm loosens and begins to unravel:

   Wind it again, checking to see that the *shel yad* is in its right place. If the *bayith* moved only slightly, no beracha is required.

TAKING THE TEFILLIN OFF

1. If one unwraps the straps of the *shel yad* all the way to the *bayith* (instead of to the wrist) before taking off the *shel rosh*:

   If the *bayith* is still secure on the arm, then just remove the *shel rosh*.

2. May one speak while taking them off?

   Yes.

3. If one takes off the *shel rosh* without first unwinding the strap around the fingers:

   Be careful next time to first unwrap the strap.

PUTTING THE TEFILLIN AWAY

1. As one winds the strap around the *bayith*, the end of the strap dangles and falls to the floor:

   It should be lifted up immediately (since it is a בזיון מצוה, degrading act).

2. If, *chas v'shalom*, they should drop on the floor *without* their protective cases:

   A rabbi should be consulted.

SOURCES

Taking out:
(1) O.Ch. 25:6, M.B. 23.
(2) *Beth Baruch* 14:77, 223–225; M.B. 40:3.
(3) O.Ch. 25:6, *Beth Baruch* 13:20.

Shel Yad:
(1) *Maasaf L'Kol HaMachanoth* 25:8, note 60.
(2) *Beth Baruch* 13:52.
(4) Ibid. 14:79.
(5) Ibid. 14:93, in the name of the *Pri Meggadim.*

The Beracha:
(1) *pashut.*
(2) Rabbi Sheinberg, *shelita.*
(3) O.Ch. 25:5, *Shaarei Teshuva*, note 5. *L'halacha*, Rabbi Sheinberg, *shelita.*

Between:
(1) O.Ch. 25:9 Rama, M.B. 32, *Bi'ur Halacha, U'ldidan.*
(3) Ibid. Beer Hetev 8.

Shel Rosh:
(1) *pashut.*
(2) O.Ch. 25:5 Rama, M.B. 21.
(3) Ibid. 27:11, M.B. 38.
(4) *Beth Baruch* 14:66.

During:
(1) M.B., O.Ch. 25:12(47).
(2) Ibid., in the name of the *Chayei Adam.*
(3) O.Ch. 25:12, M.B. 44.

Taking Off:
(1) *pashut.*
(2) *pashut.*
(3) *pashut.*

Putting Away:
(1) *Beth Baruch* 14:196.

APPENDIX III

The proper care of Tefillin

Proper care of tefillin not only increases their life span but also prevents their being disqualified for use. The following are the two major areas where special attention should be given:

Protect from extreme conditions

The two worst enemies of tefillin are heat and water. Within minutes they may cause damage such as warpage and flaking off of the paint. Therefore, never leave tefillin in direct sunlight, on radiators, in the trunk of a car, in the luggage section of an airplane, or on a window sill. One's hair should be absolutely dry before putting on the *shel rosh*.

Beware: although the plastic tefillin bag is good protection against wetness, it does increase the temperature inside the bag.

Prevent rounding of the corners

Try not to hold the corners directly. Instead, handle the tefillin from the *titura*. Make sure that the protective cases are the proper size. If the case is too large, the tefillin will rattle inside. And a case which is too small will cause excessive friction when removing and inserting the tefillin.

Shel Rosh: One of the most dangerous moments in the care of the *shel rosh* is when sliding them in and out of the protective cases. Be careful to pull the tefillin slowly *straight* out of the case even if you are in a hurry. The same applies after *davening* when returning it into the case. Also, when bowing or bending over, take into consideration your distance from the wall, *shtender*, etc.

Shel Yad: Although the danger of sliding them in and out of the protective cases is not as severe as with the *shel rosh*, you should still be just as careful. Also avoid using a shirt sleeve that is too tight, for it will rub on the top of the *bayith*. Always keep the special cardboard cover on.

NOTES

(Some of the abbreviations used below: O.Ch.= *Orech Chaim*, M.B.= *Mishna Berura*, Tos.= *Tosefoth*, Men.= *Menachoth*)

1. Tos. Men. 34b brings the first definition; Yaakov Emden Siddur p. 28 brings the second definition. See Rashi and Hirsch on *Bereishith* 48:11. The *Pri Meggadim* suggests that the root might be *paleh*, to separate (us from the other nations). The *Aruch*, however, maintains that the word tefillin is Aramaic in origin, coming from the root *tafel*, to unite, to join together. Still another use of *pilel* is found in *Yoma* 87a (to pacify).
2. Tos. Men. 34b, which also gives another definition of "looking at."
3. Ibid., *Devorim* 28:10. See Rabbenu Bachaya's commentary on this verse.
4. See Ramban in *Shemoth* 13:16 who explains how tefillin are a *zikaron* (remembrance) (as stated in his commentary to *Shemoth* 13:9):

   "...we are to lay them [tefillin] at the place of remembrance, which is between the eyes, at the beginning of the brain. It is there that remembrance begins by recalling the appearances of persons and events after they have passed away from us. These frontlets (*totofoth*) circle around the whole head with their straps, while the knot rests directly over the base of the brain which guards the memory."

68 THE TEFILLIN HANDBOOK

5. *Mitzvath Tefillin*, Shelah HaKodesh, pp. 63-64, *Ohr Tzaddikim*, p.5.
6. *Devorim* 6:4, corresponding to the third letter of HaShem's Name.
7. Ibid. 11:13, corresponding to the fourth letter.
8. *Shemoth* 13:1, corresponding to the first letter.
9. Ibid. 13:11, corresponding to the second letter.
10. See *Berachoth* 14b.
11. Based on commentary of Rabbi Velvel Heshen, *shelita*, Jerusalem.
12. O.Ch. 25:5, M.B. 15.
13. *Devorim* 6:7.
14. *Shemoth* 13:9. See *Kiddushin* 35a.
15. *Mitzvath Tefillin*: Shelah HaKodesh, pp. 64-65. Cf., *Chayei Adam* 14:27 and the explanation of the *Beth Baruch* 249.
16. See his commentary to *Shemoth*, pp. 164-165.
17. See Rashi, *Bereishith* 25:31.
18. The disagreement between Rashi and Rabbenu Tam is based on differing interpretations of a *Braiytah* discussed in the *Gemora*. See Men. 34b.
19. O.Ch. 32:44, M.B. 212.
20. Men. 36b.
21. Ibid. 37a.
22. Ibid.
23. O.Ch. 27:1.
24. Men. 37a.
25. Ibid. 37b.
26. O.Ch. 27:11 (Rama).
27. See M.B. 27:11 (47).
28. Men. 37b.
29. *Devorim* 11:18.
30. O.Ch. 27:1-2 (M.B. 9).
31. Ibid. 27:7, M.B. 18, 29.
32. Ibid. 27:4, M.B. 14.

33. *Megilla* 24b.
34. *Sanhedrin* 88b, *Kiddushin* 37a.
35. Men. 37a.
36. Ibid. 37b.
37. O.Ch. 27:10, M.B. 36.
38. Cf., *Beth Baruch* 14:65, where he concludes that although the use of a mirror is technically permitted, here the use of one's hand is sufficient (ולא ניתנה תורה למלאכי השרת).
39. Ibid. 28:1, M.B. 3.
40. היסח הדעת (forgetfulness) does not mean that one has to realize every second that he is wearing tefillin. It means that the person is occupied with what he is doing and, at the same time, senses the fear of Heaven. Primarily, light-headedness and joking around are considered היסח הדעת. Cf., M.B. to O.Ch. 44:1 (3).
40a. Men. 37a.
41. See *Ein Yaakov*, Men. 37a, *HaBoneh*.
42. See Question 11, p. 43.
43. O.Ch. 27:4, M.B. 15.
43a. *Aruch HaShulchan.*
44. *Shabbat* 49a, 130a.
44a. *Beth Baruch* 14:34.
45. O.Ch. 32:39, M.B. 176. See also Rambam's commentary to *Mishna Eruvin* 4:8.
46. Ibid. 32:40, M.B. 184; Ibid. 33:3, M.B. 19.
47. Based on *Aterath Zekenim*, O.Ch. 32.
48. *Shabbat* 108a.
49. *Berachoth* 6a.
50. *Divre HaYamim* 17:21.
51. Men. 34b.
52. Ibid.
52a. Ibid. 37a.

70 THE TEFILLIN HANDBOOK

53. Eliyahu Rabba, O.Ch. 25:5, note 8.
54. Men. 36a.
55. O.Ch. 25:11.
56. Ibid. 28:2, M.B. 6.
57. Ibid.
58. Ibid. 28:2, M.B. 7; see *Bi'ur Halacha*, beginning *Sh'lo yifgo*.
59. Ibid. 25:6, M.B. 23 explains that the reason we pass over the mitzvah is because the *posuk* clearly states to place the *shel yad* first.
60. Ibid. 28:3.
61. Ibid. 40:1.
62. Ibid. 110:4, M.B. 20.
63. Men. 36a.
64. O.Ch. 25:10, M.B. 35.
65. Men. 36a, *Sotah* 44b.
66. O.Ch. 25:10, M.B. 36, *Bi'ur Halacha, Im shama kaddish.*
67. Ibid. 25:9, M.B. 32, *Bi'ur Halacha, U'ldidan.*
68. Ibid. See *Bi'ur Halacha, V'im hifsik.*
69. Ibid. 25:7, M.B. 24.
70. *Bach.* Brought in *Maasaf L'Kol HaMachanoth* by Rabbi Y.M. Gold, p. 11, note 43.
71. O.Ch. 25:5 Rama, M.B. 21.
72. Ibid. Cf., *Aruch HaShulchan* 25:13 for another answer.
73. Cf., O.Ch. 60:4, M.B. 7.
74. Ibid. 25:12, M.B. 47. If a urinal is used, then no beracha is necessary. Today, some *poskim* are lenient in all cases. Therefore, if a regular bathroom is used to urinate and the door is left partially open, we may be lenient. (Rabbi Sheinberg, *Shelita*)
75. Men. 35b.
76. Maharsha, Men. 35b *Kesher*, *Yoma* 72b *Shelosha ze'erim*, Kid. 66a *Maaseh l'Yani HaMelech.*
77. Based on Kabbalah.

78. Hilchoth Tefillin, 3:1.
79. Men. 35b.
80. Ibid. 35a.
81. O.Ch. 33:3, M.B. 19.
82. Siddur *Minchath Yerushalayim*, p. 424.
83. O.Ch. 27:11, M.B. 38.
84. Ibid. M.B. 41.
85. Eliyahu Rabba 25:5, note 8. Brought in *Mitzvath Tefillin*, p. 123, note 2.
86. O.Ch. 32:52, M.B. 233.
87. Ibid. 27:2, M.B. 10. This *halacha* refers to the time when the tefillin are being worn. Those who want to be *machmir*, adds the *Mishna Berura*, and have the *yud*-knot against the *bayith* even when the tefillin are in their bag, should take the advice of using a thread or an extra piece of leather inserted in the *ma'abarta*. If a thread is used, one must be careful not to pass the thread under the *bayith*. Therefore, it is best to ask a reliable person to tie it. Cf., *Ben Ish Chai*, Parshath Vayera, 15, and *Eshel Avraham*.
88. Ibid. 32:44, M.B. 201.
89. Men. 35a, O.Ch. 32:44.
89a. Organizations such as *Vaad Mishmereth STaM* are available for consultation and provide guidelines to follow in this important area.
90. Ibid. 36 a-b.
91. *Shaarei Teshuva*, O.Ch. 30:2.
92. O.Ch. 30:2, M.B. 3. *Bi'ur Halacha, v'yesh mi.*
93. This period of time varies in different latitudes. In *Eretz Yisroel*, it is approximately 52 minutes before sunrise.
94. See O.Ch. 30:3, M.B. 13.
95. *Shemoth* 31:17. There are different opinions how Yom Tov is called a sign. One opinion is that the first Pesach in *Mitzrayim*, which is called "a sign," is compared to all Yomim Tovim, as it says, "And Moses

declared to the children of Israel the appointed seasons of the L-rd" (*Vayikra* 23:44). (Brought by M.B., O.Ch. 31:1 [3]). Others compared Yom Tov to Shabbat, since Yom Tov is called Shabbat. The *Pri Meggadim* suggests the source is from the *posuk* "...and let them be for signs and for seasons" (*Bereishith* 1:14).

96. O.Ch. 31:1, M.B. 5.
97. Ibid. 29:1, M.B. 2. Some authorities disagree. See also O.Ch. 31:1 and O.Ch. 308:4.
98. Ibid. 31:2 Rama, M.B. 8. The *Mishna Berura* concludes by saying that it is better not to make a beracha on the tefillin.
99. Ibid. 37:3 Rama says to begin on the day of the Bar Mitzvah. See M.B. 12 and *Bi'ur Halacha, d'Hi Katan*, where he explains why we do not follow here the Rama. Cf., *Oth Chaim V'Shalom*, 37:3, note 5, where he supports the ruling of the Rama.
100. Men. 35a.
101. O.Ch. 32:42, M.B. 191.
102. Even when a metal mold is used, some are careful to have the newly-made *shin* pushed back in completely (or in part) and then pulled out again with a pair of pliers.
103. Olath Tamid, Rabbi S. Houminer, p. 17b; *Mitzvath Tefillin,* Shelah HaKodesh, p. 71.
104. O.Ch. 32:42, Taz 35; Eliyahu Rabba 32, note 65.
105. *Mitzvath Tefillin*, Shelah HaKodesh, p. 45, note 18.
106. Eliyahu Rabba, O.Ch. 25:5, note 8.
107. *Olath Tamid*, p. 17b.
108. *Berachoth* 30b. See the *Ben Ish Chai's* explanation in his book *Ben Y'hoyada*, p. 32b. Cf., *Beth Baruch* 14:96. Also, see Rabbenu Yona's commentary to the *Gemora*.
109. The letter *shin* is on the *bayith* of the *shel rosh*; the *dalet*, in the knot of the *shel rosh*; and the *yud* is in the knot of the *shel yad*.
110. *Sefer HaChinuch*, Mitzvah 421.

Postscript

Everybody feels special when he first starts laying tefillin, and as a result he is very careful with all the rules and customs. Unfortunately, though, after a while we sometimes forget the holiness of what we are doing. To prevent such forgetfulness, Rabbi Yeshaya Heshin, *z''tl*, of Yeshivat Etz Chaim in Jerusalem, used to tell the following true story to all his students when they reached Bar Mitzvah.* And, as will be clear from reading the story, it is not just for Bar Mitzvah young men.

The Power of Tefillin Vanquishes a Plague

The European city of Ostraha was famed for its great Torah scholars and *tzaddikim*, including the Maharsha, the Yeybi Saba (author of *Morah Mikdosh*), and many others.

---

*Taken from Rabbi Heshin's book of Bar Mitzvah discourses, *Divre Yeshaya*, Jerusalem, 1954.

Once a devastating plague ravaged the city, threatening the lives of the entire population. The Chief Rabbi of the city decreed a day of fasting and prayer, hoping to arouse the Jewish community to *teshuva*. Then, once the words of the prophet would be fulfilled: "Let us search and try our ways and turn back to the L-rd," perhaps HaShem would save the city. Concerned also that the cause of the calamity may have been an irresponsible person, the Chief Rabbi announced that anybody observing anyone suspicious should immediately inform his office.

It happened that around the time that the plague began, a certain Jew stopped coming to his regular *minyan* in the morning. Everyone assumed that he was praying at some other shul. Now, however, with the heightened concern of the townspeople, curiosity was aroused, and two men were sent to investigate the matter. They followed him around the whole day but found nothing suspicious in his activities. They resolved, however, also to spy on him at night. Sure enough, at midnight they noticed that he lit a candle and made preparations to leave. He then left his house and walked along the road leading out of the city. The two men followed after him, taking every precaution to prevent being noticed.

The man walked until he came to the next town, entered quietly and vanished from their eyes. The two spies were afraid to continue further, for who knew what danger lay ahead? Instead, they returned home and, the next morning, reported their story to the Chief Rabbi. He also felt that the behavior was very suspicious but realized that there was insufficient proof.

"Tonight," suggested the Chief Rabbi, "stand watch again by his house, and as soon as he lights a candle, one of you come and inform me. I then will join you, and together we'll follow him and find out exactly what he's doing."

That night, everything happened just as the Chief Rabbi suggested. This time, however, when the man entered the second town, the Chief Rabbi and the two spies steadfastly continued after him.

They followed him until he came to a certain spot at the edge of the town and sat down by the side of an old stone wall. Then he took out a *siddur* from his bag and began saying *tikun chatzoth*, prayers recited over the destruction of the Temple. His voice was mournful and full of passion; his heart seemed to melt as he broke out into tears.

The Chief Rabbi and the two spies stood behind a grove of trees and watched him in utter silence. Their amazement grew when they suddenly heard a second voice, also chanting mournfully. There was only one man, yet they distinctly heard two voices. No matter how intently they listened or how closely they spied out the area, they remained baffled as to the source of this mysterious voice. The sound of the second voice was incomparable in depth of feeling; indeed, they had never heard anything like it.

"It's perfectly clear now," whispered the Chief Rabbi to his companions, "that this man is not a cause for our suspicions. Still, I think that we should wait here to see what he does afterwards. Also, maybe we can learn from where the mysterious voice is coming."

After the man finished reciting *tikun chatzoth*, he stood up, tied his cloth bag, and set out to return home. He had not gone far along the main road before the three secret observers came out in front of him.

"We have been following you all night," admitted the Chief Rabbi, "suspecting that you were the cause of our city's terrible plague. Now that we have seen that you are a true servant of HaShem, all our suspicions have completely vanished, and we therefore beg your forgiveness."

The man nodded his consent but made no comment.

"May I ask you one small question," continued the Chief Rabbi. "We saw you enter the town alone and recite *tikun chatzoth*; yet we heard two voices lamenting. Please tell us, whose was the second voice?"

The man answered by speaking about other topics, evading the question.

"I order you," said the Chief Rabbi sternly, "as the city's rabbi, to answer. Tell us the truth; whose was the second voice which we heard?"

When the *tzaddik* heard the strong tone of the Chief Rabbi, he confessed, "I have no choice but to reveal the truth.

"For many years now I have been accustomed to mourn over the destruction of the *Beit HaMikdosh.* My prayers caused a special response Above, and I was given a gift from Heaven. *Yirmiyahu HaNavi*, who prophesied at the end of the First

Temple and witnessed its destruction, was sent to me every night. Together, we recite the *tikun chatzoth* and lament. This is the second voice, the voice of *Yirmiyahu*, which you heard."

The three listeners were stunned. After a long moment of silence, the Chief Rabbi decided to question the *tzaddik* further.

"We realize now that you are a man of great merit to be found worthy enough to have *Yirmiyahu HaNavi* come and say *tikun chatzoth* with you. Surely your words have a great effect in Heaven. So, I wonder why you have not seen fit to stop this terrible plague. Or, if that is not in your power, at least the cause of the plague – be it a wicked person or some hidden sin – should be known to you. And if you say you don't know this either, then why haven't you asked *Yirmiyahu HaNavi*?

"And a last question," continued the Chief Rabbi curiously. "Why have you not been *davening* in shul recently?"

The *tzaddik* simply replied to the Chief Rabbi's inquiries by saying that the next day he would *daven* in shul and there he would answer all the questions. Their conversation ended as they entered the city of Ostraha. The night was almost over when they separated and returned to their homes.

After *Shacharith*, the two townsmen who had been with the Chief Rabbi could not restrain themselves from revealing the incredible tale. Soon, the whole city was alive with the news that there lived in their midst a hidden *tzaddik* and, tomorrow morning, he would be *davening* in the Central Synagogue.

Early the next morning the synagogue began to fill up, with everybody from young to old coming to see the *tzaddik*. Soon there was no more room left inside, and late-comers were forced to wait outside in the courtyard of the synagogue.

Expectation grew as the time of *Shacharith* arrived and the hidden *tzaddik* still had not appeared. The Chief Rabbi declared, however, that the morning services should not be delayed.

The congregation began *davening*, and because of the large multitude of people, the prayers echoed with great fervor. This increased intensity only heightened everyone's expectancy. Suddenly, in the middle of *Pesukei Dizimra*, the *tzaddik* arrived. His appearance as he entered the synagogue cloaked in his tallit and wearing tefillin caused great fear to spread among the congregants. Alarm and confusion replaced the passionate prayers; some men even fainted from fright.

The *tzaddik* walked straight to the front of the synagogue without seeming to notice the general panic that was surrounding him. He steadfastly made his way to a place by the front corner wall and quietly began *davening*. Slowly everyone resumed his prayers.

At the conclusion of the morning service, the Chief Rabbi came over to the *tzaddik* and said, "You have added an additional marvel to the extraordinary events of yesterday. Why did fear and confusion fill the congregation? Some fainted from fright, you know.

"Also," he added, "you promised the other night to answer in full all the questions I put before you. If you please, now is the time."

"Why the people reacted to my entrance this morning is

79

simple,'' answered the *tzaddik*. ''It says in the Torah, 'And all the people of the earth shall see that you are called by the name of the L-rd; and they shall be afraid of you.' *Chazal* interpret this verse as referring to the tefillin *shel rosh*. Therefore, tefillin have a special way of igniting awe and fear. So you see, when I entered the synagogue adorned with tefillin, everybody was afraid. The holiness of tefillin....''

''But we all lay tefillin every day,'' interrupted the Chief Rabbi, ''and yet there is never any reaction like this!''

''The reason,'' explained the *tzaddik*, ''is because I am always extremely careful never to speak *divre chol* while wearing tefillin. Also, I am careful always to treat them with proper respect, such as never walking in an unclean place. Thus, the great *kedusha* of my tefillin has never been reduced. There still remains in them the original quality which *Chazal* express: because of the tefillin all the people of the earth will fear you.

''But,'' warned the *tzaddik*, ''if a person does not properly respect his tefillin, then he diminishes their *kedusha*. By speaking *divre chol*, by being light-headed with others in shul, by even forgetting for a minute that you are wearing them – all these reduce the power of tefillin. True, the mitzvah of wearing tefillin is being fulfilled, but their awesomeness has been lost.''

He continued in a somber voice, ''You wonder why I have not been coming to shul. The reason is simply because of the way everyone conducts himself in shul. First, people do not guard the *kedusha* of their tefillin, as I explained. Second, they are not cautious in their speech, for quite often I heard even *lashon hara* being spoken. Don't they know that a synagogue is a place of great *kedusha*? I simply was not able to tolerate this type of behavior. Moreover, I was afraid that I might weaken, Heaven forbid, and accidentally be pulled into speaking *divre chol*. Therefore, I stopped coming to *daven* in shul.

"Now," concluded the *tzaddik*, "the cause of the dreadful plague in our city should be clear. People are not careful to refrain from speaking *divre chol* in the synagogue. And they are also careless in how they behave when wearing tefillin.

"If you will see fit to correct these things," he advised, "then the plague will end immediately." After he finished speaking, he left the synagogue with his tallit and tefillin held securely under his arm and was never seen again.

Everyone was dumbfounded as the *tzaddik* left, and soon a steady murmur arose from the congregation. At that point, the Chief Rabbi went up to the *bimah* and proclaimed that every member of the community should attend a general assembly to be held later that same day in the same place in order to hear what the *tzaddik* had said.

When the appointed hour arrived, the synagogue was overflowing with people. The Chief Rabbi entered, and a path was made for him as he walked to the pulpit. He spoke with great emotion, intending to arouse the congregation to the seriousness of the situation. After telling the whole story of the hidden *tzaddik*, he explained about the holiness of the synagogue and the requirement of giving it *kavod*. He continued by describing the *kedusha* of tefillin and the prohibition of speaking *divre chol* while wearing them. Then, dramatically raising his voice, he declared to his entire community, "By failing to follow these holy requirements, we have brought upon ourselves the horrible plague that has gripped our city."

Many of the people broke out into tears, and they all openly admitted their error. They took upon themselves to make a general ordinance. From then on, it was absolutely forbidden for any person to speak *divre chol* in the synagogue. The regulation applied as well to being careful in fulfilling every aspect of *hilchoth* tefillin. Later, they had engraved on a plaque in big letters: STRICTLY FORBIDDEN TO SPEAK *DIVRE CHOL* IN THIS SYNAGOGUE.

The people of Ostraha took their vow seriously, never again speaking *divre chol* in shul. Whenever a stranger came into the synagogue and, not knowing of this ordinance, began asking questions or speaking general conversation, they would not answer him. Instead, they would immediately show him the plaque hanging on the wall and then direct him outside. There, they would speak freely with him about all that was on his mind.

As soon as the people of the city accepted these rules upon themselves, the plague ceased. From that time onward, there was light and rejoicing for the Jews of Ostraha.

7 / *Climbing Har Sinai:* father and son

When the train carrying the Goldstein boys came into Grand Central Station in New York City, Sammy was stunned by the roar of the trains, the crowds of people and the blare from the loudspeakers. Without Jerry to shepherd him through the maze, he would not have had the faintest idea what to do or where to go. It was no wonder that Sammy was under strict orders not to let go of Jerry's hand even for an instant. With the assistance of dozens of people and almost two and a half hours of local travel time, they finally arrived at cousin Joshua's house. They were exhausted but exhilarated as they rang the doorbell.

"*Baruch HaBah*!" welcomed their Aunt Rachel as she opened the front door. "Look who's here, Mike." She called to her husband. "The Goldstein brothers. Long time no see. How are you, and how are your dad and mom?"

"Everyone is well, *Baruch HaShem*," answered Jerry. "May I call home to tell them that we arrived safely?"

"And don't forget your tefillin," Sammy added.

"Of course you may call," said Uncle Michael as he gave them each a hearty handshake. "But first come on in and put your things down and make yourselves at home. Josh should be home any minute, now. He went to pick up his new suit which needed some last minute alterations."

The Goldstein brothers felt at home right away and soon had their bags set aside in the basement recreation room. Joshua's younger brother and sister, Chaim and Rivka, were running all around, trying to help as much as they could. They took their visitors into the kitchen and served them sandwiches and cold lemonade. In the middle of lunch, Josh came home with packages under both arms. As soon as he saw Sammy and Jerry, he smiled and exclaimed, "*Shalom Alechem*!"

"*Alechem Shalom*!" they returned happily.

Sammy was really excited to see his cousin and good friend. Within minutes after *benching*, they were sitting together in Josh's bedroom, catching up on the year in which they had not seen each other. Josh showed Sammy his tefillin, his new suit and hat and other things which he had received for his Bar Mitzvah. They felt naturally close to each other and spent a good part of the afternoon and evening together.

The next morning was *erev* Shabbat, and everyone was very busy. Besides the normal Shabbat preparations and the *kiddush* in shul, there was the mitzvah of welcoming the many out-of-town relatives who had come for this important occasion. Since the various accommodations had been prearranged, most everything was going very smoothly.

"Hi, Dad!" shouted Sammy when he saw their car drive up. "What took you so long? It's nearly 2:30."

"Oh, we had some things to do on the way," his father answered as he got out of the car. "By the way, don't let me forget to give Jerry his tefillin later. Okay?"

"Sure, I won't forget."

As Shabbat approached, the fathers and sons walked to shul for *Kabbalath* Shabbat and *Maariv*. *Zeide* Katz was telling everyone about his Bar Mitzvah in the Old Country over fifty years ago. With his dramatic nature, he made the story a classic retelling of HaShem's miracles and *chesed* as he escaped from Europe before World War II. Later, during the joyful Shabbat meal, together with *zemiroth* and *divre Torah*, the reunion between the two families felt complete.

The following morning, everybody went off to shul with a happy spirit and a deep sense of gratitude to the Almighty. The Goldsteins sat opposite the *bimah* a row behind Mr. Katz, Josh, Chaim, and *Zeide* Katz. When the time came for the *Sefer Torah* to be taken out of the Ark and to be read, everyone felt the excitement in the air. Mr. Katz was called up for the first *aliyah* of *kohen*. As the *baal koreh* read the *sedrah*, the congregation quietly followed along in their *chumashim*. Between each *aliyah*, there was time to talk while the *mi-sheberachs* were being said.

While their father was speaking with a relative of the family, Jerry turned to Sammy and said, "Being called up for an *aliyah* is really something special, isn't it?"

"It looks a bit scary to me," commented Sammy.

"Just wait 'til you're called up for your first *aliyah*," Jerry spoke reassuringly, "and then you'll understand what I mean. When you stand in front of that big, open *Sefer Torah* and say *asher bochar bonu mi-kol ho'amim, v'nothan lonu eth Toratho...* 'Who has chosen us from among all the other nations and given us His Torah...,' you'll feel the great joy and importance of being a Jew."

"What do you mean?" asked Sammy. "I already say *asher bochar bonu* every morning."

"Sure you do. But you haven't climbed up to the *bimah* and held a real *Sefer Torah* in your hands and said it. Have you?"

"No, not yet," he admitted. "So tell me then: what's it all about?"

" 'What's it all about,' " repeated Jerry quietly, "Well, I can't say I know what it's *all* about, but I remember being scared and proud and...."

Just then it came time to call up Josh for *maftir*, and the *chazan* sang in an announcing tone, "*Ya'amod, HaChatan, HaBar Mitzvah* Yehoshua b'Reb M'chel *HaKohen, Maftir.*"

Joshua was excited and nervous as he ascended the *bimah* with his father's *tallit* draped over his shoulders. He held the wooden handles of the open *Sefer Torah* and recited *asher bochar bonu* in his boyish voice. After the congregation enthusiastically answered *amen*, Joshua carefully sang the *maftir*. At this point his father came over to the *bimah*, waited until Josh finished the after-beracha and then said the beracha *sh'patorani* without *shem u'malchuth*.

A few minutes later, when Josh was chanting the *haftorah*, Sammy watched him with delight. With a very clear, sweet voice, he sang the *haftorah* smoothly and accurately, showing that he had prepared his lessons well. Sammy was very proud of his cousin and very happy for him.

After *davening*, there was a *kiddush* in honor of the Bar Mitzvah, with lots of *mazel tovs*, handshakes, family and friends' reunions, songs and words of Torah. There was a call for silence as the rabbi of the shul, Rabbi Leiberman, was about to speak. He stood up and, with a broad smile, expressed the congregation's joy at participating in this *simcha* of Mr. and Mrs. Katz and their first-born son Joshua. He continued by bringing up the subject of *Shavuoth*:

> *Shavuoth* is only a few more days away, and Joshua is about to enter this *chag* for the first time as a Jew obligated to do the mitzvoth. Actually, there is a very interesting connection between *Shavuoth* and Bar Mitzvah. The Chasam Sofer explains that both the Jew on *Shavuoth* and the young man on his Bar Mitzvah share a common, hidden mitzvah — the mitzvah of rejoicing. This joy exists as the person accepts upon himself the yoke of HaShem's mitzvoth.
>
> This mitzvah, however, is hidden because when the Torah tells us to rejoice on *Shavuoth*, it is referring to the festival of first fruits, the holiday of the wheat harvest. It is natural that we should be happy when celebrating our physical success. But the Torah never refers to *Shavuoth* as the holiday of *Matan Torah* and, therefore, the mitzvah of rejoicing is not expressly directed to this aspect of the holiday. And how could it? HaShem would not command us to rejoice at the same time when we are accepting the yoke of the Torah

on our shoulders. With all these new responsibilities and obligations, a person is not expected by HaShem to feel in the mood of rejoicing.

Still, from our point of view, in order to be found worthy of accepting the yoke of Torah, we ignite the joy from within ourselves. We freely take upon ourselves the task of stirring up this spiritual rejoicing. As a result we come to the real purpose of the holiday, which is not to be happy just because of the plentiful food but because of *Matan Torah*, which brings freedom to our soul and joy to our spirit. We realize that material things serve only as a means, not as an end. By happily accepting the yoke of the Torah, we taste the real happiness of life.

The same is true of the mitzvah of rejoicing on the day of the Bar Mitzvah. Suddenly, like a big yoke upon his neck, the Bar Mitzvah young man is responsible for fulfilling all the *Taryag mitzvoth*. How could he be ordered to be happy at a time like this? But once he realizes that the mitzvoth were given him for his good, with only his best interests in mind, then he can ignite from within himself a response of joyfulness. So, we see how both *Shavuoth* and the Bar Mitzvah day share the same hidden mitzvah of rejoicing — the key to the day's success.

Rabbi Leiberman paused and seemed to look at all the faces of the Bar Mitzvah-age boys in the audience.

Actually, — he continued — there are many other ways for the Bar Mitzvah young man to feel this special joy. One way is to appreciate the greatness of what he is doing. When, for example, Joshua climbed up the steps of the *bimah* this morning, he was not just climbing steps. The *bimah* is compared to *Har Sinai*. So when he went up on the *bimah*, he was climbing up the spiritual steps to receive and read the Torah — the direct words of HaShem.

Then he said the all-important *berachoth* which affect the quality of our *kavannoth* as we do the mitzvoth.

The first beracha begins in the past tense, "who chose us...and *gave* us His Torah," but ends in the present tense, "Blessed are You, HaShem, who *gives* the Torah." Why in the same beracha do we change from past to present tense?

One explanation is that the Torah which we received at *Har Sinai* is not some ancient relic now put away in the *Aron HaKodesh*. On the contrary, the Torah is given to each and every one of us daily — anew. This idea means that when we sit down to study Torah today, we are able to discover new avenues of thought and come close to feeling the greatness of the Torah as our forefathers did at *Har Sinai*.

Following the Torah reading, a second beracha is recited: "...who has given us the Torah of truth and has planted eternal life in our midst...." This beracha does not say *His* Torah as was said in the first beracha. Rabbi Yaakov Emden points out that between these two *berachoth* is the reading from the *Sefer Torah*. Before we involve ourselves in the Torah learning, the Torah is HaShem's alone; so the first beracha says "His

> Torah." But once we have read the Torah very carefully and have made its truth part of our being, then the Torah is no longer exclusively HaShem's but ours as well. We have become partners with HaShem — a very important and exciting enterprise!
>
> We hope that these few words will help Joshua and all of us to feel that special spark when we learn Torah and live our Jewish way of life.

Rabbi Leiberman then looked over at Mr. Katz and continued:

> It is interesting to note that while the father stands on the *bimah* when his son is publicly proclaiming his allegiance to Torah and mitzvoth, a slight change takes place in the role which the father plays in bringing up his son. The beracha *sh'patorani* — "who has freed me from the punishment of this child" — signals the direction of the new relationship.
>
> Many *poskim* explain the beracha in this way: Until now, the father was duty-bound to instruct his son in the mitzvoth and guide him along the path of truth. If, however, the father neglected his duty, then *he* is held responsible for the errors of his son. Now that his son has reached Bar Mitzvah and carries the responsibility of his future on his own shoulders, the father publicly announces their new relationship. From now on, he is free from any punishment which his son deserves for not learning and doing the mitzvoth properly.
>
> Although the father, technically speaking, is free from the mitzvah of *chinuch*, he still has a guiding hand

in his son's activities. If he sees his son doing something wrong, it is his right and duty like every other Jew to voice his disapproval and to take any necessary steps to correct the situation. And if he fails to do so, then he is held responsible.

After a short pause, Rabbi Leiberman concluded his speech.

Certainly all of us know the fine Torah tradition that the Katz family represents. Zeide and Bubba Katz have done so much to raise their family and build our congregation. And you Mr. and Mrs. Katz, the parents, have worked a labor of love to bring your son safely to this bench mark of Jewish manhood. In fact, I can recall Joshua's *brith milah* here in our shul and the *simcha* then. Today, we see before us the first realizations of the aspirations which you, Mr. Katz, voiced on that occasion. *B'ezrath HaShem*, may the coming years bring you continued *nachas* as your son matures in the ways of Torah knowledge and the sincere fulfillment of the mitzvoth. And may we be together with you under his *chupah*, as well as at the *simchoth* of all your other children. In conclusion, there is a *minhag* mentioned in the time of *Chazal* to bring the Bar Mitzvah young man before the leaders of the community to be blessed.

Rabbi Leiberman turned to Joshua.

We have watched you grow up from infancy into young manhood with all the qualities of Torah excellence maturing in you like fruit ripening on a *rimon* tree. Just as the bud which opens into a small berry-sized fruit and only slowly grows to full size and sweetness, so, also, have you shown your parents, family and teachers that the potential within you as a child has reached a new stage of development. Of course, we are very pleased that you are continuing in your path of Torah commitment by going on to *yeshiva ketannah* in the fall. With this plan for the future, may *HaKadosh Baruch Hu* bless you to develop into a completely ripe *rimon* full with seeds of mitzvoth and good deeds. And in this way bring your parents and all of *Am Yisroel* real Yiddishe *nachas*.

Rabbi Leiberman shook Joshua's hand and then Mr. Katz and Zeide Katz's hands as everyone started singing *simon tov u'mazel tov*.

Joshua's birthday came out this year on *Motzei Shabbat*. So, after a joyous Shabbat, Josh and his father and younger brother walked to shul with the Goldsteins to *daven Maariv*. They were a few minutes early, and only three or four shul members had arrived ahead of them. One of them jokingly said to Mr. Katz, "So you've brought a *kosher l'minyan*-maker with you! Great!"

"Are you referring to my nephew, Jerry Goldstein, from Baltimore?" grinned Mr. Katz.

"By the way, Josh," mentioned Mr. Katz as he walked over to his son. "Since tonight is your birthday and everything you do from now on is as an adult, you should be sure to have in mind *birkath haTorah* when you say *ahavath olam* before *Kiriyath Shema*. Some *poskim* hold that the beracha you made this morning on learning Torah does not apply to you once you become thirteen, which is tonight. So be sure to have intention for *birkath haTorah* while saying *ahavath olam*. Also, right after *Maariv*, be sure to learn some Torah. Tomorrow night, at this time at your Bar Mitzvah *seudah*, you won't have to have this *kavannah* specially in mind."

"I hope I will be able to have anything in mind then," smiled Josh.

"Don't worry. Remember what Rabbi Leiberman said: you are a ripening *rimon*! I'm confident that your *drash* will come out as sweet and clear as ever. Now it's time for *Maariv*. Please hand me a *siddur*, Josh."

The next morning, the Katzs and the Goldsteins went together to shul for *Shacharith*. Mr. Katz patiently helped Josh put on his new tefillin. Some families have the *minhag* to start wearing tefillin a month or more before the Bar Mitzvah, but the custom of the Katz family was to wait until the very day itself. Since it was his first time, everything felt awkward to him. He had studied the laws of tefillin well and had been carefully watching others to see how they put on their tefillin. Now, at last, Josh was bringing his studies into action.

Joshua was wearing his new suit for the first time. Now, with his tefillin properly on him, he said the beracha of *shehecheyanu* שֶׁהֶחֱיָנוּ on the suit. His father had reminded him beforehand that, when saying the beracha, he should have in mind also the tefillin, as well as all the mitzvoth which he would fulfill for the rest of his life. Suddenly, the beracha "...that He has kept us in life and sustained us and has enabled us to reach this time" gave very special meaning to this moment. Joshua said it with emotion, and those who were gathered around answered *amen*.

Sammy noticed how self-consciously Josh behaved

throughout the *davening*. He was always touching his tefillin to make sure that they were still in their right place. Josh's eyes twinkled, and when he noticed Sammy looking at him from across the aisle, he gave him a little wink. Sammy was so excited that he wished that he could put on tefillin right then and there.

8 / *The royal banquet*

☙ On Sunday evening, many of the Katzs' relatives and guests gathered in a nearby banquet hall where the special Bar Mitzvah meal was beautifully prepared. There were many tables with lovely flowers and decorations and, of course, the most delicious food. In the middle of the long head-table behind a huge *challah* was seated Joshua — the guest of honor. Beside him sat his father, grandfather, Rabbi Leiberman and other distinguished guests.

But Joshua did not stay seated very long since he was getting up all the time to receive everyone's handshake, *mazel tov* and — quite obviously — Bar Mitzvah present. Throughout the hall were heard toasts of *l'chaim* and *mazel tov*, and the lively spirit was enhanced by the music of a four-piece band.

Everything was in the finest taste, and no expense appeared to have been spared.

Sammy was sittting with his father and brother and was very happy. "I want my Bar Mitzvah celebration to be just like this," he announced proudly to his father.

"*Im yirtzeh HaShem*, Sam. You'll have a very fine *simcha*, too. But you should know that not all parents can afford such beautiful celebrations. My Bar Mitzvah *seudah*, for instance, was small and very, very modest compared to this. Your grandfather wasn't wealthy, you know. Today, it's the in-thing: big and fancy!"

Mr. Goldstein fingered the spoon in his hand. "Did I ever tell you about the Bar Mitzvah celebration I went to in Mea Shearim in Jerusalem?"

"I don't think so."

"Well, about two years ago when I was in Israel, a series of events led me to one of the most special Bar Mitzvah *simchoth* I've ever attended.

"One day, when I happened to be in Geula, a section of Jerusalem, I decided to take the Number One bus to the Kotel to *daven Mincha-Maariv*. At the bus stop was a short, elderly man wearing one of those wide-brimmed *Yerushalmi* hats. He kept looking down the street to see if the bus was coming. He glanced at me and asked me what time it was, and I felt that he must have been in quite a hurry or else that the bus was running very late. As we spoke, he told me that he was worried that if the bus did not come soon, he would be late for *Mincha* at the Kotel. When I offered to take him with me in a taxi, he shrugged his shoulders and kept waiting for the bus. Another

EGGED 1
1 אגד

minute or two later, the bus came, and we happened to sit next to each other.

" '*Baruch HaShem*,' I began, 'there will be plenty of time for *Mincha*, won't there?'

" 'I hope so,' he said. 'Eliyahu *HaNavi* was answered at *Mincha*. So you see, it's a special time to *daven*, particularly at the *Kotel HaMaaravi*.'

" 'Yes, the *Kotel* is a very special place.'

" 'It's the *makom hakodesh* where all our *tefilloth* go up to Heaven.'

"As the bus approached Jaffa Gate of the Old City — still some distance from the Western Wall — a huge traffic jam was before us. After five minutes, I went up to the driver and asked him to open the door so that we could walk to the *Kotel*, but to my surprise he refused. Several other passengers also failed to convince him until my companion went up and whispered something in his ear. Immediately, the driver opened the doors, and whoever wanted to get off did so. I was a bit amazed at how he succeeded so easily and asked him what he told the driver, but he said only that it was getting late for *Mincha* and we had better walk fast.

"As we approached the Wall, several people recognized my companion and came over to greet him. It then seemed to me that certainly he was no ordinary man. My curiosity increased when I couldn't find him after *Mincha*, and only by accident did I notice him sitting deep inside the Wilson's Arch, which is along the side of the *Kotel*. I asked him if I could bring a chair and talk with him, and his silent nod of approval was enough for me to quickly find a chair. Soon, he guided the conversation into the importance of thoroughly fulfilling the mitzvoth, and the need to learn even about those mitzvoth which we are unable to fulfill today — like those connected with the *Beit HaMikdosh*.

" 'But don't think that there are only *Taryag mitzvoth*, my friend,' he said smiling. 'Really, there are many more mitzvoth, each with a source from a verse in *Tenach*. Many people don't realize this, so much so in fact, that a number of years ago I decided to collect them in a series of books called *Eved HaMelech*. Have you seen them?'

" 'No.'

" 'Well, if you would like to drop by my house on the way home tonight, I'll be happy to show them to you.'

"Rabbi Houminer — I had asked him his name — lived in *Batei Natan* which is next to Mea Shearim. He had a small room full of his books, a truly incredible set on the whole *Tenach*. I selected several volumes to buy from him, and we sat down at a small table in his living room. I call it 'his living room' for your sake, Sammy. Actually, it was a large room with a table in the center and several beds and a small corner desk where we sat. In that room he ate, slept, learned and wrote. I'll always remember his bright, happy eyes and his kindly voice.

"While we were talking, a child of about nine or ten years came in and gave my host an envelope. After opening it, he looked at the card inside, spoke a few words with the boy and then turned to me.

" 'This,' he explained, 'is an invitation to a Bar Mitzvah reception from one of our neighbors. The young man's grandfather lives upstairs and is a *dayan* on one of the local religious courts, and the Bar Mitzvah boy himself is full of great potential. Perhaps, if you will still be in *Eretz Yisroel* next week, you would like to come and join me.'

"I, of course, accepted and was delighted to have an excuse to meet this great Torah personality again.

"The following week, I was on my way to *Batei Natan* when I decided to stop in a bookstore and buy a gift for the Bar Mitzvah boy. I asked the shopkeeper what he recommended for such an occasion, and he offered several suggestions. I told him that this was the first time I was going to a Bar Mitzvah celebration in Israel and I didn't know quite what to expect.

" 'Here, in our circles,' he said as he leaned over the counter, 'it's not lavish at all. It's not at all like in America.'

" 'Which circles do you mean?'

" 'Torah circles. It's a different atmosphere altogether.'

" 'Okay. I'll report back to you, *b'li neder*, my findings and impressions.'

"A young yeshiva man who had overheard our conversation came over to me and asked, 'By any chance are you going to so-and-so's Bar Mitzvah tonight?'

" 'I believe I am. Why?'

" 'Well, I'm also going and am looking for a gift. I don't want to get the same *sefer* as you select.'

" 'Where do you know the family from, if I may ask?'

" 'Oh, the Bar Mitzvah boy's grandfather is quite famous here in *Yerushalayim*. Don't you know?'

" 'No, I'm sorry to say. I'm just visiting from the States.'

" 'I see. Anyway, I go to him with questions pretty often, especially over the last several years.'

"He showed me which *sefer* he had selected and excused

himself, saying that maybe we would see each other at the *simcha*.

"When I got to *Batei Natan*, Rav Houminer greeted me, 'So you were able to come, my friend. Very good.'

"Together we walked from his house through the *shuk* in Mea Shearim to the huge *Talmud Torah* building across from the *shtibel'ach*. He was telling me that many *Talmidei Chachamim* had received their early education in this *Talmud Torah*. As we walked up the wide staircase along with others, I was surprised to see that people were leaving and coming downstairs. The *simcha* was being held on the second floor in the children's dining hall, which had been divided for men and women. The hall was very noisy and full of people when we entered. We walked over to the front table where the guests of honor were, shook the Bar Mitzvah boy's hand and presented him his gifts. The father and grandfathers greeted us, and we were immediately offered a tray of what looked like home-baked cakes and cookies. Though a stranger, I was given a royal welcome. Everyone at the head-table was wearing what seemed to be his best Shabbat clothes, and the atmosphere was light-hearted and joyous.

"Rav Houminer and I found places to sit down on a bench, and someone started talking with him. In the meantime, I took in the scene with amazement. No band to liven up the hall; no waiters to serve a seven-course meal; no fancy chandeliers hanging from high ceilings with fine draperies and lush carpets. Instead, some boys were in charge of bringing out new bottles of drinks and more cakes and nuts. Everything was simple and pure. The community was sharing this happy occasion with the Bar Mitzvah young man and his family. The goal was not to eat as much as you could. The goal was to proclaim the entrance of a new member into the Jewish community.

"Still, I was bothered by one question. Perhaps the reason everything was so simple was because of financial limitations. I gave my seat to someone else to sit down and went over to stand near the wall. The young yeshiva man whom I met in the bookstore came over to me, and in our conversation I soon brought up the question with him.

" 'As far as I know,' he answered, 'it's more a question of emphasis than an issue of finances. Here, the emphasis is on Torah scholarship and moral perfection. Clothing, food and shelter are all essentials; luxuries, however, are not. This Bar Mitzvah young man is beginning the path of adulthood with a proper sense of values, learning already that he must use modestly the money which HaShem has given him. Certainly an unfancy but pure *simcha* like this one will better train qualities of Jewish holiness and righteousness than a rich, showy affair. Don't you also think so?'

" 'I can't help but agree with you. This whole event is making quite an impression on me, and thank you for your comments.'

"That was my first and only encounter with a *Yerushalmi* Bar Mitzvah, and to this day it is still engraved in my mind.

"Actually, there's an interesting postscript to this story," continued Sammy's father. "Before I left Israel, I visited the *Kotel* one more time, and as it happened, I met Rabbi Houminer again and, of course, thanked him again for taking me along to the Bar Mitzvah. But I was still very curious to know what he had told the bus driver to get him to open the door.

"After I pressed him for the answer as politely as I could, he revealed that he had told the driver simply that he wanted to make *Mincha* in time at the *Kotel* and that, by helping, the driver would be like a partner in the prayers. The driver immediately opened the door and asked if his son, who was in the army, could also be included in the prayers. Rabbi Houminer's eyes were full of peace as he told me that whenever we Jews see our goals coming together, then automatically things work out for the better.

"So you see, Sammy, reaching Bar Mitzvah and becoming a full-fledged member of the Jewish community are really serious business. By the way, based on this episode, your mother and I have been thinking seriously that your Bar Mitzvah party should be simple, but with *kavod*. But we'll talk more about this later."

Across the table sat Rabbi Levi. He was a teacher in one of the finest *Talmud Torahs* in Brooklyn and a long time friend of the Katz and Goldstein families.

"I couldn't help overhearing your story," said Rabbi Levi, "and I think that you are very right. The *seudah* is important, but it's more important to realize your new responsibilities to HaShem and the Jewish people. If we would remember that our righteous forefathers also made Bar Mitzvah *seudoth* for their sons, then perhaps we would behave more in their spirit of *kedusha* and modesty.

"*Chazal* tell us that Avraham *Avinu* made a Bar Mitzvah *seudah* when his son Yitzchak was weaned. The *posuk* says, 'And the child grew and was weaned. And Avraham made a feast on the same day that Yitzchak was weaned.' We usually understand the word 'weaned' as Rashi does to refer to a time when the child is two years old and no longer dependent on his mother's milk. But the *Midrash* interprets it differently: the word 'weaned' means being weaned away from the *yetzer-harah*. Thus, according to this *Midrash*, Yitzchak was thirteen years old and had just been given his *yetzer-tov*. Therefore, the rest of the *posuk* — 'and Avraham made a great feast' — is telling us about Yitzchak's Bar Mitzvah celebration, which Avraham prepared for the occasion."

"That's very interesting," Mr. Goldstein commented. "Most of us know about the *seudah* at the *brith milah*, but we don't realize the importance of the Bar Mitzvah *seudah*."

"This is certainly true," agreed Rabbi Levi. "In fact, even the *Zohar* goes into the topic with a whole story about Rebbi Shimon Bar Yochai — the Rashbi — and his son Elazar. Once the Rashbi invited the leading *chachamim* to a festive meal, without specifying the purpose of the *simcha*. The whole house was decorated in the finest way possible. He had the *chachamim* seated on one side of the table while he sat opposite them on the other side.

"The Rashbi was in a state of great happiness, his face radiating joy. They asked him, 'Rabbenu, why are you happier today than on other days?' He smiled and answered, 'On this day a holy soul has descended on angel's wings into my son Elazar. With this banquet my joy is complete.' At that moment Elazar was brought to his side, and the Rashbi said to him, 'Sit down, my son, sit down. On this day, the day of your Bar Mitzvah, you have become sanctified and your lot is with the *tzaddikim*.'

"And as a final point," continued Rabbi Levi, "did you

know that *Chazal* even compare this *simcha* with a wedding celebration?"

"I suppose," answered Mr. Goldstein, "because both are levels of maturity, both are steps in becoming a man."

"Precisely. If I recall, the source for the comparison is the *posuk* in *Shir HaShirim*. 'Go forth, O daughters of Zion, and behold King Shlomo with the crown with which his mother crowned him on the day of his wedding, and on the day of the gladness of his heart.' A *Tanna* asked, 'What does it mean, "the day of his wedding?" ' And another Tanna answered, 'On the day when he becomes capable of doing the mitzvoth of the Torah.' 'When is that?' 'From thirteen years and older. On that day he should participate in his Bar Mitzvah *seudah* with a joyous heart just as he should participate in the *seudath* mitzvah of his own wedding with a joyous heart.' This is the similarity between the two."

"Very well put."

Sammy listened quietly during their conversation while he glanced around the banquet hall. Some of Josh's friends were dancing in a circle along the far side of the hall, and Jerry got up to join them. Suddenly, Sammy turned to his father and said, "But Dad, Jerry had a big, fancy Bar Mitzvah. Josh is having one and so will all my classmates, too. I also want one. How could I face them if I don't get the very best? Jerry's Bar Mitzvah was with all the extras, and I'm entitled to the same treatment. Aren't I?"

Mr. Goldstein put his arm around the back of Sammy's chair. "I know Jerry had a royal Bar Mitzvah celebration. That was before I went to *Eretz Yisroel* and decided to re-examine my ideas and values."

"Jerry always gets the best," Sammy's inner feelings burst out. "He's always first. First in this, first in that. It's not fair. And without a real Bar Mitzvah party I simply won't be able to face my friends. It's simply not fair."

"Sammy," gently replied his father, "Sammy, I understand what you're saying, and it's valid to a point, but only to a point. However, now is not the time to have a full discussion on the issue. Let's make Joshua feel good at his *simcha* and later when we return home, we'll talk further. Okay, Sammy?" Mr. Goldstein gave Sammy a big hug, and Sammy felt better as he went over to join the dancing.

Rabbi Levi commented to Mr. Goldstein, "Dovid, I don't envy you in this very touchy situation. How do you plan to handle it from here?"

"Well, first I need a lot of *siyaita d'shemaya.*"

"Of course."

"Then, after Sammy and I have a really good talk, I'm thinking of having Jerry join us. Maybe, if they can each voice their feelings together, things will resolve themselves."

"Sounds good to me."

"Ladies and gentlemen," rang a voice over the microphone. "Ladies and gentlemen, may I please have your attention."

Mr. Katz, acting as master of ceremonies, was standing by his son at the head-table. He was adjusting the height of the microphone and tapping on its head to be sure that it was working. The band stopped playing, and the boys who were dancing started returning to their seats.

"It is a great honor," Mr. Katz announced as the noise in the hall died down, "to have you all join with us tonight at our *simcha*. Our Sages tell us that a *seudath mitzvah* is only complete when it is accompanied by words of Torah. How great an honor it is for me to introduce our son, Yehoshua, and to ask him to say a *dvar Torah*. Please,..."

There was a round of applause as Joshua stood up. His father lowered the microphone and placed it in front of him. Joshua smiled but felt nervous with so much attention focused on him. On the table in front of him were notes of the *drash* which he and his father had worked on together.

"My dear parents, grandparents, rabbis, guests and friends," Joshua said in a very soft voice. Everyone was quiet, some turned their chairs in order to face the head-table. Mr. Katz whispered to Joshua to speak more directly into the microphone.

"My dear parents, grandparents, rabbis, honored guests and friends!" he repeated in a louder voice. "I want to thank you all for coming tonight and joining in this *simcha*.

"It is customary that the Bar Mitzvah boy says a *dvar Torah*. I have chosen to speak about the mitzvah of tefillin, and I hope that you will find it interesting."

Joshua picked up the paper with the notes as he cleared his throat.

"It says in the *Midrash Shachar Tov*, 'Yisroel said to HaShem: "Our desire is to toil in the study of Torah by day and by night, but we cannot because we have to work for a living and do not have free time." HaShem replied: "By fulfilling the mitzvah of tefillin, I shall credit you as if you toiled in the Torah by day and by night." '

"Based on this *Midrash*, we can ask a very basic question:

What is the power of tefillin that, by wearing them, one is credited with learning Torah all the time?

"To begin with," Joshua paused and glanced at his notes, "in order to answer this question, we must understand first what are the benefits of studying Torah. If we think about it, we would see two main benefits. One: by studying Torah we learn the right path to follow in life and the right way to fulfill the mitzvoth. This is what *Chazal* say, 'The learning of Torah leads one to doing the mitzvoth properly.' To achieve this benefit, a person could learn *halacha* until he knew the basic requirements and not necessarily have to study Torah all day and night.

"Yet there is a second benefit which can be achieved only by learning Torah all the time. We all know that a person has a *yetzer-harah* from birth. Rashi, in fact, brings this in the eighth Chapter of *Bereishith* on the verse, 'The inclination of man's heart is bad from his youth.' The word 'youth' in Hebrew is *na'ar*. Rashi explains the phrase 'from his youth' as from the time he stirs out, *n'na'er*, from his mother's womb. As of that time a child is given his *yetzer-harah*.

"The job of the *yetzer-harah* is to pull us away from the right path. One of the best weapons we have against it is the Torah, and only by constant study, can we be victorious. This is what the *Gemora* says in *Kiddushin* 30b: 'G-d said to Israel: "My children, I created the *yetzer-harah* and I have created the Torah as its antidote." ' Torah learning is like a bandage that prevents the wound of the *yetzer-harah* from getting worse. As long as we are studying, we are protected. But once we stop learning, the *yetzer-harah* returns to cause us much pain and pulls us away from the right path."

Joshua paused and looked briefly around the packed hall and then quickly at his notes. It was better not to see so many people.

"Now," he continued after strengthening his courage, "we can return to the *Midrash*. The children of Israel spoke out, 'Our desire is to study Torah all day and night since we must be strong against the *yetzer-harah*.' HaShem answered them, 'Wear tefillin and I will credit you with constantly studying Torah since tefillin act on a person to instill in him good character traits and fear of Heaven.' And as we know, the best weapons against the *yetzer-harah* are good *midoth* and fear of Heaven.

"The Rambam writes at the end of the fourth chapter of *Hilchoth Tefillin*, and these are his words, 'This holiness of tefillin is very great since, as long as a person is wearing them on his head and arm, he is humble and has fear of Heaven, nor does he become light-headed or speak vain things.' Tefillin, which in the time of *Chazal* were worn all day, was a shield against the *yetzer-harah* all the day.

"And even today when we wear our tefillin for only a short amount of time in the morning during our prayers, we still can receive its protective benefits throughout the entire day. How? The *Sefer HaChinuch* discusses the protective shield given us by reciting the *Kiriyath Shema* once in the morning and once in the evening. In Mitzvah 420, the *Sefer HaChinuch* says that the *Shema* that we say in the morning protects us all the day long, and the *Shema* that we say in the evening helps protect us throughout the night. Similarly, we can say that the tefillin which we wear in the morning protects us all day long. And since we do not wear tefillin at night, by saying *Kiriyath Shema* at *Maariv*, we have the merit of learning at night and gain protection from the *yetzer-harah*.

"Now that I have just started wearing tefillin and will go on to *yeshiva ketannah* to learn more Torah, I pray HaShem will help me to use the weapons He gave me to win the battle against the *yetzer-harah*. I want to thank HaShem for bringing me to this all-important day in my life. Also to my parents for taking care of me and giving me a Torah education. And to my teachers and rabbis for helping me feel a deep love of Torah and mitzvoth. And to all you honored guests: May we all be worthy to see the *Moshiach* soon."

Joshua sat down as applause filled the banquet hall. Mr. Katz gave his son a hearty handshake, followed by Rabbi Leiberman, who was sitting on the other side of Joshua. The band began playing a happy tune, and everyone started talking and resuming his meal.

Mr. Goldstein was speaking with Rabbi Levi at their table when he looked up and said, "Well, look who's coming this way! The honored father of our new Bar Mitzvah young man! And he's bringing a *l'chaim* with him for the occasion."

Mr. Katz had started going from table to table to have a *l'chaim* with his guests. A photographer with a sound-video camera was following him, getting everyone at each table on tape. As he approached their table, Mr. Goldstein stood up and gave him a hearty handshake. "A big *mazel tov*, Mike, to you and your whole family."

"Thank you, my dear friends," he replied as he shook everyone's hand. "And to each of you a *l'chaim tovim u'lshalom!*"

That evening's *simcha* marked a special time for everyone. But for Mr. Goldstein it also marked a public declaration of his feelings — feelings which he hoped that his son Sammy would also understand.

9 / *On eagles' wings*

☙ As the Goldstein family drove back to Baltimore the next morning, Sammy was full of mixed feelings. On the one hand, he was on eagle's wings: cousin Josh's Bar Mitzvah seemed to have gone by in a flash. He was simply excited about a lot of things: *Matan Torah*, tefillin, growing up more. On the other hand, he felt confused about the prospects of his own Bar Mitzvah party.

"Sammy," his father called as he glanced into the rear-view mirror. "Why don't you take a nap? I know you didn't get much sleep last night and you really need the sleep."

"I can't."

"I know," sympathized his mother. "But why don't you try anyway."

"I'm thinking about so many things all at once. I couldn't get my 'computer' to slow down even if I wanted to."

"What affected you the most, Sammy?"

"Um, I don't know. A lot of things. On the good side, I guess I'll always remember the way Josh looked at me with his tefillin on. He was super!"

"By the way, Sammy, pretty soon you'll have to set aside a few minutes every night to learn the laws of tefillin."

"Yes, Dad. Rabbi Adler already talked to me about it."

"Good. By the way, did Mom mention to you that your tefillin were ready? We picked them up on the way out to the Katzs."

"Wow! Let me see them."

"Shuuu," whispered his mother, "you'll wake up Jerry."

"You'll have to wait until we get home, Sammy. They are packed away. But I'll tell you, they are truly *mihadrin min hamihadrin* — the very best. I wouldn't mind having a pair like that myself."

"Thanks so much, really! This is the best Bar Mitzvah present of all! When can I start wearing them?"

"There's still time, Sammy, don't worry; they won't fly away! I was thinking that maybe Jerry would start learning with you — he could use a brush-up himself."

"Wait a minute, now!" popped up Jerry. "How do you know?"

"We thought you were sleeping," his mother looked at him in surprise.

"I was just making a fatherly guess," answered Mr. Goldstein. "By the way, Jerry, when was the last time you looked at *hilchoth* tefillin?"

"At my Bar Mitzvah."

"That was over three years ago. I don't think it would be such a bad idea for you to take a little brush-up course. You'd get the mitzvah of teaching Torah, too."

"I'll think about it. I'm really so busy."

"That's just the kind of person I'm looking for. You know the old saying: if you want to get something done, ask a busy person."

"*B'li neder.*"

"Great," smiled Sammy. "Let's get started right away."

"Hold your horses," asserted Jerry. "You don't have to leave the starting gate before everybody else. The invitations to your Bar Mitzvah haven't even been printed yet. By the time of your *simcha*, I won't be surprised if you'll be able to teach me a few things too."

Sammy's joy was suddenly sobered. "Oh, Dad wants to give me a poor man's Bar Mitzvah."

"I beg your pardon," Mr. Goldstein objected, "but I never said that to you. What I said, Sammy, was that since my feelings have changed after my trip to Israel and you, however, want a big *simcha*, therefore, we have to sit down and discuss it together when we get home."

"I didn't know," said Mrs. Goldstein as she looked at her husband, "that you had mentioned anything to Sammy yet."

"Last night the subject came up," he replied, "and perhaps this would be a good time to continue the discussion. Actually, I'm interested in knowing what Jerry has to say about all this."

"Well, Dad. I don't know what to say. Everybody likes a fancy Bar Mitzvah. Mine was great. But the story you told us about Jerusalem certainly shows that so much fanciness may not be so necessary."

"But what will my friends say?" objected Sammy. "And all the presents I'll be missing out on? Jerry always has better than me!"

"Now hold on," answered Mr. Goldstein. "Did I say that you were not going to have a Bar Mitzvah party at all? I just said that it was going to be more modest and less showy. If we Jews have been blessed with financial success, how will we be able to justify in *Shemayim* the use of money for over-indulgence? Don't we — HaShem's Chosen People — represent a different view of life and a different way of living?"

Mr. Goldstein drove the car into one of the rest stops on the turnpike. Everyone got out to stretch his legs and take a break. Jerry took Sammy aside and said, "You know, Sammy, it's not easy to understand what Dad is talking about. But maybe we should agree because he thinks so."

"I like the word 'we.' It's *my* Bar Mitzvah party!"

"Aw, come on Sammy. You'll have plenty of presents. And whatever's missing, I'm sure Dad will make up to you."

"But my friends. What will they say?"

"Who's more important: your friends or your father? Besides, think how Dad and Mother have to consider *their* friends, and they're not worried. If we look at things honestly, aren't most of the guests at a Bar Mitzvah friends of the parents? Some of these uninvited guests might even be insulted for not being invited. Yet Dad and Mother are willing to face what might happen in order to follow through with what they believe is right."

Sammy turned away momentarily and looked at the cars

driving along the turnpike. What's really at stake? he thought to himself. My honor. But so is the honor of my parents at stake. I have to admit, Jerry really made a very good point. If Dad and Mom are willing to leave *their* honor aside, then I should be able to do the same. The only question is: can I stick to my guns and gulp down my pride face-to-face with my friends? I just don't know. I know what should be — but what really will be, I just don't know.

"Jerry, what you say seems right," Sammy responded as he turned back towards his brother, "but to tell you the truth, I don't know if I can conquer my *yetzer-harah* which keeps telling me: no, don't give in."

"Humm," Jerry grinned. "If that is the only thing between you and a whole-hearted acceptance, then maybe we can come up with an idea that will help."

"What?"

"Let me think. What will make your *yetzer-harah* content? Humm. Oh, yes. Yes, I've got it!" Jerry said excitedly. "Dad said there'll be a party — a modest one — but still a real Bar Mitzvah party. Right? Well, then, even though only a few of their friends are being invited, maybe they might agree to let you invite *all* of your friends. How many do you have in your class? Twenty-five? Thirty? I don't know where they are planning to make the party, but even if it is in the house I think there will be space for everybody. What do you say to this?"

Sammy thought for a minute. "You know, Jerry, your idea sounds not so bad. But do you think Dad and Mom would agree?"

"I don't know," answered Jerry, "but we can...."

"Hurry up boys," shouted Mr. Goldstein from the car. "We're all set to go."

The brothers gave an earnest look at each other and then, together, walked in the direction of their parents.

"I didn't know," said Sammy, "that growing up was such hard work. Listening to other people, making difficult decisions, fighting the *yetzer-harah*. It's a full-time job."

"Now you know," said Jerry. "The real battle is just beginning. But, with HaShem's help, you have a way to win."

"I wonder if I can do it," sighed Sammy. "Yes, I just have to do it," he added hopefully.

Annotated Glossary

Biographical Sketches

Annotated Glossary

NOTE: (1) Letters in brackets are the plural endings or the possessive form.
(2) Hebrew phrases are listed under the first letter of the first word. For example: *mazel tov* is listed under M.
(3) Dates in parenatheses refer to the secular calendar, B.C.E. (Before the Common Era) or C.E. (Common Era).

A

aat-bash: See footnote, p. 104.
Abba: father.
Acharonim: later rabbinical authorities, beginning with the publication of the *Shulchan Aruch* (c. 1550 C.E.), and continuing until today.
Admor (אדמו״ר): abbreviation for:
אד׳=אדונינו : our master
מ׳=מורינו : our teacher
ור׳=ורבינו : and our rebbe
Title given to Chassidic Rebbe.
ahavath olam: everlasting love; opening words of the blessing which comes before the *Shema*. See *Berachoth* 11b.
ahavah (*-at*): love (love of).
after-*beracha*: blessing recited after eating a certain quantity of food or drink. Cf., *benching*.
Alechem Shalom: welcome; said in response to *Shalom Alechem*.
alef (א): first letter of the Hebrew alphabet.
aliyah: to go up; to be called up to the *bimah* to recite a blessing over the *Sefer Torah*.
Am: people.
Amoroim (singular, *amora*): literally, interpreter. The Torah sages beginning with the death of Rabbi Yehuda HaNassi (218 C.E.) and ending with the death of Ravina (498 C.E.). The period began with the compiling of the *Mishna* and ended with the completion of the *Talmud*. They labored at explaining, interpreting, and understanding the *Mishna*.
arba-esre: fourteen.

Arba Minim: four species (*etrog, lulav, hadas, aravah*) shaken during *Sukkoth* (Festival of Booths). See Lev. 23:40.

Aron Kodesh: Holy Ark, containing the *Sefer Torah*. It is placed in the shul along the wall facing *Eretz Yisroel*.

asher bochar bonu: "who has chosen us;" from the beracha recited daily before learning Torah and before reading from the *Sefer Torah* in shul.

Ashkenaz (*-im*): the Jewish communities of Germany, many immigrating northeast into Poland and Russia, and later to England and America. Cf. *minhag*.

Avinu: our (fore-) father. There are three Forefathers (Patriarchs): Abraham, Issac and Jacob. Cf., *Berachoth* 16b.

avodah (*-ath*): work, service.

Avoth (pl.): Fathers; specifically, the Patriarchs. Cf., *Avinu*.

B

baal koreh: reader of the *Sefer Torah*.

baalei teshuva (pl.): repentants, i.e., someone who does a transgression and then regrets his deed, confesses it, resolves never to do it again and in not never does it again; also used to refer to someone who although fact raised observantly, discovers his Jewish heritage and thereafter keeps Torah and mitzvoth. See *Berachoth* 34b.

Bar Mitzvah: lit., "son of the commandments"; age of Torah obligation; in law, an adult responsible for his acts.

Baruch Hashem: Blessed is G-d.

Baruch Habah: welcome; lit., "blessed is your coming."

baruch shem kavod: "Blessed be His name, whose glorious kingdom is for ever and ever." Recited in a whisper after saying "Hear O Israel, the L-rd our G-d, the L-rd is One." Cf., *Pesachim* 56a.

batei: houses of.

bayith (pl. *batim*): house; in tefillin, "compartment," the place where the Torah inscriptions are inserted. Cf., tefillin.

b'chor: first-born.

bechirah: free choice, free will; "I have set before you life and death, blessing and curse; choose life" (Deut. 30:19).

beit (ב): second letter of the Hebrew alphabet; two.

Beit HaMidrash: lit., house of study. Cf., *yeshiva*.

Beit HaMikdosh: The Temple; lit., the House of Holiness. The First Temple was built by King Solomon in Jerusalem in 832 B.C.E. and stood for 410 years. After the seventy year Babylonian exile, the Second Temple was built by Ezra and his Beit Din. It was destroyed 420 years later by Titus in 68 C.E. See *Seder HaDoroth*.

benching: (Yiddish) lit., bless; specifically, the grace after meals.

Bemidbar: Book of Numbers; lit., "In the desert."

beracha (-oth): blessing(s).

Bereishith: Book of Genesis; lit., "In the beginning."

b'ezrath HaShem: with the L-rd's help; customarily added in conversation to indicate the need for HaShem's help in all of man's activities or plans; "Happy is he who has the G-d of Yaakov for his help" (Psalms 146:5).

bimah: lit., platform; a centrally located table, often elevated, on which the *Sefer Torah* is placed when being read.

birkath haTorah: special blessings recited daily in the morning prayers before learning Torah; also referring to blessings recited publicly when reading the *Sefer Torah*. See *Berachoth* 11b. Cf., *asher bochar bonu*.

b'li neder: lit., without taking a vow.

Bnei Noach: Gentiles; lit., children of Noah. They are obligated in seven commandments: (1) not to serve idolatry, (2) not to blaspheme the name of G-d, (3) not to kill, (4) not to commit adultery, incest, etc., (5) not to steal, including kidnapping, (6) not to eat a limb taken from an animal before it has completely died, (7) to establish laws and judicial procedures. Cf., *Sanhedrin* 56b.

Braiytah: traditions and opinions of *Tannaim* which were not included in the *Mishna*. Cf., *Mishna, Tannaim*. Lit., external, outside.

brith milah: covenant of circumcision. For a healthy infant, the circumcision takes place on the eighth day. See Gen. 17:9-14.

C

chacham (*-im*): Torah Sage; lit., wise man; of any generation including the present. Cf., *Chazal*.

chag: festival, holiday. The three main festivals are Passover (*Pesach*, 15-21 Nisan), Weeks (*Shavuoth*, 6 Sivan), and Booths (*Sukkoth*, 15-21 Tishre). See Lev. Ch. 23, Num. 28:16-29:39, Deut. Ch. 16.

chaim: life.

challah: bread baked specially to be served on Shabbat and holidays, usually braided or shaped specially. On Shabbat two loaves are used as a memorial to the manna which our forefathers ate in the wilderness, as it says, "And it came to pass on the sixth day they gathered *twice* as much bread" (Ex. 16:22).

chametz: leavened bread. Forbidden throughout the seven days of Passover. See Ex. 12:17-20. Symbolically, the Evil Inclination: just as the leaven (yeast) causes the dough to rise, so the Evil Inclination rises in the thoughts, words and deeds of a person and causes him to stumble. Cf. *yetzer-harah*.

chas v'shalom: Heaven forbid.

Chassid (*-im*): Lit., pious person; generally, the disciples of the Baal Shem Tov (1703-1763); today, many Chassidic dynasties have branched out, such as Lubavitch, Ger, Belz, Breslov and Satmar, each with their own rebbe, traditions, customs and writings.

chatunah: wedding.

Chazal (חז"ל): Torah Sage, specifically *Tannaim* and *Amoroim*, who are mentioned in the *Talmud*. An abbreviation for:

ח' = חכמינו : our wise men
ז' = זכרונם : may their rememberance be
ל' = לברכה : for a blessing

Cf., *chacham*.

chazan: cantor, leader of the prayer service.

chesed: kindness, generosity; "The world is built by *chesed*" (Psalm 89:3).

chet (ח): eighth letter of the Hebrew alphabet.

chinuch: education, child rearing. "Educate a child in the way he should go, and when he is old he will not depart from it" (Proverbs 22:6). Cf., *Kiddushin* 29a.

Chol HaMoed: intermediate days of the Festival of Passover and the Festival of Booths; lit., the profane [days] of the festival. These days have more holiness than an ordinary weekday, Hallel is sung, most shops are closed, and festive meals are served.

Chumash (*-im*): Five Books of Moses; the Pentateuch; from the Hebrew root *chamesh*, five.

chupah: wedding canopy.

Chutz L'aretz: lit., outside the land [of Israel]. "The Land of Israel is holier than all other lands. In what way is it holier? Only from the Land of Israel are brought the *Omer* offering, the first-fruit offerings, and the two-loaves offering of *Shavuoth*" (*Mishna Kellim* 1:6).

D

dakoth: lit., thin, lean; in tefillin, a method of making tefillin using small pieces of leather and gluing them into the appropriate shape (the *bayith*). A thin piece of leather is then attached to the whole outer surface. Cf., *peshutim, gassoth*.

dalet (ד): fourth letter of the Hebrew alphabet.
daven (*-ing*): (Yiddish) pray.
dayan (*-im*): rabbinic judge.
Devorim: Book of Deuteronomy; lit., "These are the words."
divre chol: everyday conversation.
divre Torah: words of Torah; a speech on a Torah topic.
drash: explanation of a Torah topic; sermon, homily.
dvar Torah: lit., words of Torah; short *drash*.

E

echod: one.
Eliyahu: Elijah. See I Kings, ch. 17 — II Kings, ch. 3.
emunah: faith, trust.
Eretz Yisroel: the Land of Israel. "Rabbi Shimon bar Yochai said: 'G-d gave three goodly gifts to the Jewish people, each entailing suffering — Torah, *Eretz Yisroel* and the World to Come' " (*Berachoth* 5a). *Eretz Yisroel* is called "A land flowing with milk and honey" — milk flowing from the goats, and the honey flowing from the dates and figs (*Megilla* 6a; Rashi, Ex. 13:5). Cf., *Ketuvoth* 112a.
erev: evening, eve of.
Eved HaMelech: lit., servant of the king; title of a commentary of all of *Tenach* by the late Rabbi S. Houminer.

F

frum: (Yiddish) Torah observant Jew.

G

Gadol HaDor: the Torah leader of the generation.
Gaon: lit., genius; generally, the heads of the Babylonian academies from 590 C.E. to 1037 C.E.
gassoth: method of making tefillin whereby the whole *bayith, titura* and *ma'abarta* are all made from a single piece of leather; introduced in large part by Rabbis A. Sofer and Nathanel Tefilinski (1870-1945).
gedolim: Torah leaders.
gematria (*-ioth*): method of explaining the Torah based on the numerical value of Hebrew letters and words. For example, Rashi uses *gematria* to explain the meaning of the message Yaakov sent to Esav, "I have sojourned [גרתי] with Laban, and stayed there until now" (Gen. 32:5). The *gematria* of גרתי is תרי"ג. The implication of Yaakov's message was:

"Although with the evil Laban I sojourned [גרתי], the תרי"ג *Taryag mitzvoth* I kept, and thus I didn't learn to copy his bad ways."

Gemora: lit. completion (of the talmudical discussions on the *Mishna*), teachings; the discussions and debates on the *Mishna* in the academies of the *Tannaim* and the *Amoroim*, which themselves were put into writing; divided into sixty tractates. Cf., *Amoroim, Tannaim*.

Geula: lit., redemption; also, name of religious neighborhood in Jerusalem.

gezerah shava: analogy; a method of deriving a law whereby a comparison is made between two identical words in Scripture. Since the law is such-and-such in the first instance, in the second the law must be similar. A *gezerah shava* is valid only when it has been received by tradition from an earlier *Tanna* or *Amora*.

guf: body.

guf naki: lit., a clean body; in *halacha*, the capacity to control not passing gas while wearing tefillin, reciting the *Shema* and praying the *Shemone Esre*. Cf., *Orech Chaim* 37:2-3; 80:1.

H

haChatan: the bridegroom; a young man.

haftorah: lit., to leave, to end; the section read from the Prophets — containing some reference or idea from the weekly Torah portion — following the Shabbat reading from the *Sefer Torah* and sung in a special melody. Historically, it began as a replacement for the Torah reading when the Greeks under Antiochus (150 B.C.E.) forbade all religious books. The Books of the Prophets were permitted because they were considered history books.

Haggadah: lit., the recitation, the telling; the book read at the Seder on Passover. "And you shall tell to your son on that day, saying, 'It is because of that which the L-rd did for me when I went out from Egypt' " (Ex. 13:8).

HaKadosh Baruch Hu: The Holy One blessed be He.

halacha (*hilchoth*): lit., to go, thus, teaching the way to go, as it says, "You shall make known to them the way in which they must go" (Ex. 18:20); the law.

halacha l'Moshe m'Sinai: laws which are not based on a source from a verse, nor can they be derived from logic; rather they are known as coming directly from Moses who heard them from G-d.

HaNassi: the Prince; title of the Torah leader of the generation who sat at the head of the *Sanhedrin Hagadolah*.

HaNavi: the prophet; prophecy ended at the beginning of the Second Temple with the deaths of the Prophets Haggay, Zechariah, and Malachi (318 B.C.E.).

har: mount, mountain.

HaShem: lit., "The Name"; G-d.

hei (ה): fifth letter of the Hebrew alphabet.

I

im yirtzeh HaShem: if HaShem wills. Cf., *b'ezrath HaShem*.

ish: man, adult.

K

Kabbalah: mystical part of the Torah; lit., transmitted. See *Chagiga* 11b.

Kabbalath Shabbat: welcoming in the Shabbat; the custom is to read Psalms 95 to 99, sing *L'cha Dodi*, and recite Psalms 92 and 93. The custom originated in Safed during the lifetime of Rabbi Moses Cordevero (c. 1540 C.E.).

kaddish: lit., sanctification; special prayer recited only with a *minyan* (1) by the *chazan* as part of the order of the daily service, (2) by a mourner during the first eleven months after the death of a parent, (3) after learning Torah in a group. It was composed at the beginning of the Second Temple by the Men of the Great Assembly in the new language acquired by the Jews during the Babylonian exile, Aramaic. Based on the verse, "I will magnify and sanctify Myself, and I will make Myself known in the eyes of many nations, and they shall know that I am the L-rd" (Ezek. 38:23).

kadesh kol bachor: to sanctify every first-born male.

kal v'chomer: form of logical argument; Example: We learn that one should touch his tefillin often with a *kal v'chomer* from the gold plate (*tzitz*) worn on the forehead of the High Priest. Scripture states that when he is wearing the gold plate, which has the name of HaShem engraved in it, he should always realize that he is wearing it. Tefillin, which have many times the name of HaShem written inside them, all the more should the wearer be conscious that he is wearing them and touch them often (*Menachoth* 36b).

kametz: vowel mark (ָ).

kanfe yona: wings of a dove; just as a dove uses her wings for self-protection, so Israel is protected by the mitzvoth which it does (*Shabbat* 49a).

kavod: honor, dignity.

kavannah: intention; the mental concentration on the purpose and meaning of a mitzvah in order to enhance its quality; tying together the action of the mitzvah with its deeper meaning.

kedusha: lit., holiness; part of the service in the repetition of the *Shemone Esre* where everyone must stand, feet together, and say in unison "Holy, holy, holy is the L-rd of Hosts; the whole earth is full of His glory," etc., in fulfillment of the mitzvah "I will be hallowed among the children of Israel" (Lev. 22:32).

Kehunah: Priesthood; Cf., *kohen*.

kibud av v'em: honoring one's father and mother; Cf., *Kiddushin* 32-33.

kiddush: lit., sanctification; usually, the ceremony inaugurating the Shabbat and Yom Tov with the blessing recited over a cup of wine.

Koheleth: The Book of Ecclesiastes, written by King Solomon, who also wrote the Book of Proverbs and the Song of Songs.

kohen: priest; a descendant of Aaron, as it says, "the priesthood shall be theirs (Aaron and his sons) for a perpetual statute" (Ex. 29:9). The *kohenim* performed the service in the Temple.

kosher: lit., fit; permissible by Jewish law.

Kotel HaMaaravi: Western Wall; known also as the Wailing Wall; the only wall of the Temple not destroyed by the Romans; the place where the Divine Presence will always remain and where all prayers ascend, as it says, "How awesome is this place! This is none other than the house of G-d, and this is the gate of Heaven" (Gen. 28:17). Eleven levels of stone are visible today with seventeen levels underground.

Kiriyath Shema: lit., the reading of "Hear," i.e., "Hear, O Israel, the L-rd is Our G-d, The L-rd is One." This is one of the 613 mitzvoth, to recite the *Shema* morning and night, as it says, "And these words...shall be in your heart...and you shall talk of them...when you lie down and when you rise up" (Deut. 6:6-7).

L

lashon hara: slanderous or derogatory talk; "You shall not go about as a talebearer among your people" (Lev. 19:16).

l'chaim: to life; usually, said as a toast in honor of a person or occasion.

l'chaim tovim u'lshalom: to a good life and peace.

leining: (Yiddish) reading; generally, reciting from one of the 24 books of Scripture according to the proper musical notations.

l'shem shemayim: lit., "for the sake of heaven"; Cf., *tzaddik*.

l'shem yechud: lit., "for the sake of the unification (of His Holy Name)"; generally, a prayer which describes the significance of the mitzvah and which is said before performing the mitzvah. Cf., *kavannah*.

M

ma'abarta: lit., to pass through; in tefillin, the side through which the strap fits.

maamer: saying or discussion on a Torah subject.

Maariv: evening service; Yaakov established *Maariv* (*Berachoth* 26b); Cf., *tefillah*.

Maftir: the one who reads the *haftorah* and says, at least, the last three lines of the Torah portion. Cf., *haftorah*.

makom hakodesh: the holy place; "Take off your shoes from your feet, for the place on which you stand is holy ground" (Ex. 3:5).

Makoth: lit., lashes; the tractate (*Gemora*) dealing with the laws punishable by lashes. See Deut. 25:1-4.

malachim: angels; on Shabbat evening, for everyone who says *Viy'chulu* ויכלו ("The heavens and the earth were finished"), the two ministering angels that escort him home place their hands on his head and say, "Your sin is taken away, and your misbehavior is forgiven" (*Shabbat* 119b).

Malchuth: kingship; "Then you shall place a king over you, whom the L-rd your G-d shall choose" (Deut. 17:15); divided into the Kingdom of Judah (the House of David) and the Kingdom of Israel during the reign of Solomon's son. The exile of the ten tribes (the Kingdom of Israel) took place between the years 573 B.C.E. and 555 B.C.E. The legitimate heirs were the Kings of Judah, the descendants of King David, who was promised "Your throne shall be firm forever" (II Sam. 7:16).

Matan Torah: the giving of the Torah; usually referring to the Festival of Weeks. See Exodus, chs. 19-20. Cf., *Shavuoth*.

matzah: unleavened bread, eaten during the seven days of Passover; called "the bread of affliction"; the symbol of humility (because of its lack of rising) and freedom, as it says, "And you shall observe the commandment of *matzah*; for on this very day have I brought your hosts out of the land of Egypt" (Ex. 12:17). Cf., *Pesach*.

mazel tov: congratulations, good luck; "Where do we know that Israel is not governed by the forces of the constellations? From the verse, 'And He took him (Abraham) *out*side...'(Gen. 15:5). Abraham said, 'O Master of the Universe, I have studied my astrological chart and have calculated that I am unable to have a son.' HaShem answered him, 'Go out from your astrological calculations because Israel is not governed by the constellations.' " (*Shabbat* 156a).

Mea Shearim: lit., a hundred measure (Cf., Gen. 26:12); name of a religious district in Jerusalem; founded in 1875 as one of the first settlements outside the walls of the Old City.

Megilla: lit., scroll, a tractate (*Gemora*) dealing with the laws of Purim and the reading of the scroll of Esther.

Menachoth: lit., meal-offerings; tractate (*Gemora*) dealing with those parts of the Temple service which included the meal-offering, as well as the main talmudic discussions on the commandments of tefillin and *tzitzits* (fringes).

mensch (*-im*): (Yiddish) man, grownup, someone who behaves maturely and intelligently.

michilah: forgiveness; since the fast of Yom Kippur does not atone for sins against another human being, one must ask the person directly for forgiveness. See *Orech Chaim* 426:1.

mida (*-oth*): character trait, behavior; "All of G-d's service is dependent upon the improvement of one's character... The prime purpose of man's life is to strive constantly to break his bad traits. Otherwise, what is life for?" (Vilna Gaon, *Even Sh'lema*)

midrash: lit., explanation, interpretation; explanations of the Torah from the Tannaic period, sometimes using parables or true-life stories.

mihadrin min hamihadrin: lit., the finest of the fine; the very best; strictly kosher; carefully keeping all the minute laws.

mihudar: finest, best, choicest.

minhag: custom; the accepted practice of a family or place; therefore, one prays the same *nusach* (version) that his father uses; today there are three major *minhagim*: Ashkenaz, Sephardi and Chassidic (also called Sephard or *minhag Ari*). The historical development of these *minhagim* dates back to the ancient Palestinian and Babylonian customs which differed on many points. The Palestinian Jews, for example, finished the reading from the *Sefer Torah* once every three years instead of once a year and counted the *Omer* by day as well as by night. Over the generations, as the Jews dispersed abroad throughout the Mediterranean countries and Europe, the Babylonian *minhagim* became supreme, encountering many changes along the way. Usually, the Sephardim follow the ruling of the *Shulchan Aruch* and the Ashkenazim and Chassidim follow the ruling of the Rama (who was an Ashkenazi). The *minhag* Chassidim (called *minhag* Sephard because they adopted many points from the already existing Sephardi rite) was called *nusach* Sephard in order to distinguish it from *nusach* Ashkenaz (although it radically differed from the true Sephardi *siddurim*). The Lubavitch siddur was the first Chassidic siddur to be published and was closely based on the order set down by the Ari Zal. Cf., *siddur*.

minyan: ten adult men (at least 13 years of age) make up a minyan which permits the prayer service to include *kaddish, kedusha*, and the reading from the Torah.

mi-sheberach: lit., "He who blessed"; the opening words of a prayer said after an *aliyah* to the Torah for (1) the one who made the Torah blessings, (2) a woman after childbirth, (3) someone who is ill, (4) the rav of the shul, wife, family, friends, etc.

Mishle: Book of Proverbs, composed by King Solomon.

Mishna(-yoth): the codification of the Oral Law collected and arranged by Rabbi Yehuda HaNassi and universally accepted in 218 C.E. Divided into six orders: (1) Seeds, (2) Festivals, (3) Women (marriage, divorce, vows, *Sotah*), (4) Damages (including civil and criminal law, *Avoth*), (5) Sacrifices (in the Temple), (6) *Tahoroth* (laws of purity). "Who can you find who can successfully wage the battle of Torah? One whose hands are full with bundles of *Mishna*" (San. 42a). Cf., *Gemora*.

Mishna Berura: title of Rabbi I.M. Kagan's (*Chofetz Chaim*) commentary to the *Shulchan Aruch, Orech Chaim*, written between 1875 and 1900 and accepted as the most authoritative halachic *sefer* today.

Mishkan: Tabernacle; built in the desert by Divine decree (see Exodus, chs. 25 to 28, 35 to 39) and the focal point of the spiritual life of the Nation. In *Eretz Yisroel* it stood 450 years (24 in Gilgal, 369 in Shilo, and 57 in Nov and Givon) and was hidden away by King Solomon when he built the Temple. The Ark, Tablets, the jar of manna, and many other vessels were hidden away by King Josiah forty years before the destruction of the First Temple.

mitzvah (*-oth*): commandment, Divine decree; there are 613 mitzvoth from the Torah (see *Makoth* 23b-24a) and seven *mitzvoth d'Rabbonim* (Hallel, Megillath Esther, Channuka lights, Shabbat candles, washing hands before eating bread, blessing before eating and before doing a mitzvah, making an *Eruv*). Although there are many more *mitzvoth d'Rabbonim*, these seven begin their beracha with "who has sanctified us with His mitzvoth and commanded us...." "There is one mitzvah that is central and fundamental and upon which all the other mitzvoth depend. This is the mitzvah of learning Torah since by learning a person will know the mitzvoth and fulfill them" (Intro., *Sefer HaChinuch*).

mitzvah min hamuvchar: a commandment performed in the best way.

modeh ani lifanecha: "I give thanks unto You, O King, who lives and endures, who has mercifully restored my soul to me; great is Your faithfulness"; the first words uttered upon awakening each morning, even before washing hands.

Moshe Rabbenu: Moses, our teacher.

moshol: parable; the inner meaning of the *moshol*, its real significance, is called the *nimshol*.

Moshiach: Messiah; lit., the anointed one.

Motzei Shabbat: after-Shabbat, Saturday night; at this time a special meal (*M'lavah Malka*) is served in honor of the departing Shabbat Queen and the hoped-for arrival of the Messiah who, for various reasons, is not allowed to come on Friday or Shabbat.

mussar: character improvement, moral instruction. "Hear, my son, the *mussar* of your father, and do not forsake the Torah of your mother" (Proverbs 1:8). Cf., *Pirke Avoth*.

N

nachas (also, *nachat*): contentment, pleasure, satisfaction.

navi: prophet; "The L-rd your G-d will raise up to you a prophet from your midst...to him you shall hearken" (Deut. 18:15). Cf., *HaNavi*.

negel vasser: (Yiddish) water for washing hands immediately upon waking up in the morning.

ner: candle.

Nisan: First month in the Jewish calendar; the name is Babylonian in origin, brought back by the Jews when they returned to Israel from the Babylonian exile; see Ex. 12:2.

nusach: version; liturgy; Cf., *siddur, minhag*.

n'velah: carcass of an animal which died from (1) old age; (2) a sickness; (3) an accident; or (4) as a result of improper slaughtering. A practical difference between *n'velah* and *t'refeh* is that a *n'velah* carcass when being carried (even if not touched, i.e., on boards) causes a level of impurity to come upon the carrier. A *t'refeh* carcass, however, does not. Cf., *t'refeh*.

O

ohr: light, eve of.

Omer: a quantity of flour offered in the Temple, first offered on the 16th of Nisan from barley and thereby permitting the eating of the new crops from the five species of grain; also referring to the mitzvah of counting the *Omer* which is said every night from the 16th of Nisan until the eve of *Shavuoth*, as it says, "And you shall count for yourselves...from the day when you bring the *Omer*...you shall count fifty days" (Lev. 23:15-16).

Orech Chaim: See *Shulchan Aruch*.

P

pasach: Hebrew vowel sign (ַ).

parsha (*-iyoth*): chapter, section; section read from the *Sefer Torah* on Shabbat. "Whoever reads the *parsha* (twice with the *Targum*) week after week will live a long life" (*Berachoth* 8b).

perek Chelek: the eleventh chapter in the tractate of *Sanhedrin* which begins with the word, *Chelek* (lit., portion), and declares: "All Israel has a portion in the World to Come."

perush: explanation, commentary.

Pesach: Passover, the festival of our deliverance from Egypt; See Ex. chs. 12-15, Lev. 23:4-8, Deut. 16:1-9; celebrated from the 15th to 21st of Nisan. Cf., *matzah, chametz.*

Pesachim: tractate (*Gemora*) dealing with the laws of Passover; the name of this tractate is written in the plural (*Pesach*-im) to hint to the first *Pesach* offering on the 14th of Nisan and the second *Pesach* offering on the 14th of Iyar (Me'iri, introduction to commentary on *Pesachim*).

peshutim: lit., simple, simplified; used in reference to a method of making tefillin in which small pieces of leather are glued together into the proper shapes. Cf., *dakoth, tefillin.*

Pesukei Dizimra: lit., Verses of Song; the first section of the morning prayers, composed mostly of Psalms. Cf., *siddur.*

pilel: to argue, to think out.

Pirke Avoth: Chapters of the Fathers; *Mishnayoth* of ethical and moral teachings, found in most *siddurim* after the Shabbat afternoon prayers. The first *Mishna* opens "Moses received the Torah at Sinai" in order to emphasize that the sages of the *Mishna* said their moral teachings not as did gentile moralists who taught their own personal opinions of good and bad behavior. Rather, these *Mishnayoth* of *mussar*, like all the *Mishnayoth*, were given at Sinai to Moses (adapted from Rav Bertanora).

poskim: rabbinical authorities; the rabbinic authority of Samson in his generation (i.e., the great sages in every generation) was like Aaron in his generation.

posuk (*-im*): verse from Scripture.

posul: unfit, invalid.

Purim: festival on the 14th of Adar commemorating our deliverance from Haman during the Babylonian exile.

R

Rabbenu: our teacher, our master.

Rabbonim: lit., rabbis; synonymous with *poskim*.

reb: honorary title by which any Jew can be called; as opposed to "Rabbi" or "Rav" or "Rebbe" which are honorary titles used for certain distinguished persons in Torah and Chassidic circles.

rebbe: generally, title of the leader of a Chassidic dynasty. Cf., *Chassid*.

rebbeim: rabbis, teachers.

retzuah (-oth): strap.

rimon: pomegranate; one of the seven types of fruit that *Eretz Yisroel* is praised by in the *Chumash* (Deut. 8:8); "Even the simplest Jew is full of mitzvoth like a *rimon* (which according to tradition has 613 seeds)" (*Eruvin* 19a).

Rishonim: the rabbinical authorities from the end of the Gaonic period (1037 C.E.) until the expulsion from Spain in 1492. Including such Torah giants as the Rashi, Rambam, Baale Tosefoth, and the Rosh.

S

saas: joy, happiness.

Sanhedrin: court of law; name of tractate (*Gemora*) dealing with courts, judges, and punishments. There are three categories of judicial courts: (1) a court of three judges, which decides cases of monetary claims, theft, crimes punishable by lashes, as well as declaring the new month; (2) *Sanhedrin Ketannah* of 23 judges, which decided cases punishable by death; (3) *Sanhedrin Gadolah* of 71 judges, the highest court, which convened on the Temple grounds in the Chamber of Hewn Stone. This last court decided special cases punishable by death such as a false prophet and a high priest accused of murder. Also, it voted whether or not to go out to war.

Seder: lit., order; generally (when capitalized) refers to the reading from the *Haggadah* on Passover night, along with the four cups of wine, the matzah, and bitter herbs. Cf., *Haggadah, Pesach, matzah*.

sedrah: order, portion; usually refers to the portion of the *Sefer Torah* read in shul on Shabbat. Today the *Sefer Torah* is divided into 54 *sedrahs*, and the *minhag* is to complete them all in one year. Cf., *Sefer Torah, minhag*.

sefer: book, scroll.

Sefer Torah: Torah scroll containing the five Books of Moses. Each word was given by G-d through Moses to the Jewish People and of utmost holiness. If a single letter is missing, the *Sefer Torah* is unusable until it is corrected. The scroll is made of parchment (*klaf*) specially prepared for this mitzvah and sewn together with sinew thread. It must be lined with an instrument that leaves only an impression and written by a competent *sofer* with special ink. Each "book" is separated by four blank lines.

Sephard (*-im*): lit., of Spanish descent; today including Jews originating from all the Mediterranean countries, as well as Iraq, Iran and India. Cf., *minhag, Ashkenaz.*

seudah (-ath): meal, dinner.

Shabbat: "Remember the Sabbath day, to keep it holy" (from the Ten Commandments, Ex. 20:8). "Shabbat said in wonderment: 'Master of the Universe, to each day of creation You gave a partner (1st-4th, 2nd-5th, 3rd-6th, each pair having similar things created therein), but for me there is no partner!' The Holy One blessed be He answered her: 'The Jewish People shall be your partner!' " (*Midrash Rabba*).

Shacharith: lit., morning; usually, morning prayers, instituted by Abraham (*Berachoth* 26b), and which are to be completed during the first three hours of the day ("since this is the manner of kings to get up at three hours in the day" — *Berachoth* 9b). Cf., *tefillah*.

Shalom Alechem: lit. peace unto you; welcome.

Shas (ש״ס): the Talmud (*Mishna* and *Gemora*); An abbreviation for:

שתא = ש׳ : The six

סדרי = ס׳ : orders (of *Mishna* together with their commentaries, the *Gemora*).

Shavuoth: the Festival of Weeks, commemorating the giving of the Torah at Mount Sinai on the 6th of Sivan; On *Shavuoth* Rabbi Yosef asked specially to be served calf meat, commenting, "If not for this day (indicating that I have learned Torah and have been improved by the learning — Rashi), then how many people are there in the market place who are called Yosef (and what is there to distinguish me from them, i.e., improved)" (*Pesachim* 68b). See *Shabbat* 86b-89a.

Shechem: name of city 40 miles north of Jerusalem. See Gen., ch. 34.

shehecheyanu: lit., who has kept us in life; from the blessing "...who has kept us in life and has preserved us and has enabled us to reach this season," recited on (1) tasting a new fruit for the first time in the season, (2) on purchasing new vessels, land and property, (3) upon wearing a new garment, (4) on fulfilling a mitzvah that comes at appointed seasons. Cf., *Orech Chaim* 225.

shekel: ancient currency equivalent in value to 3.4 oz. of pure silver; called also *sela'im*; see Num. 18:16 (for redeeming the firstborn) and Ex. 30:13 (for the per capita half-*shekel* given to the Temple every year).

shel rosh: lit., of the head; referring to the head tefillin; tefillin *shel rosh* have more holiness than the *shel yad* because it has four compartments instead of one and because it has the letter *shin* on two sides.

shel yad: lit., of the hand; referring to the hand tefillin.

shelita (שליט״א): title of honor and blessing (mentioned after the name) for a living person. Abbreviation of:

שיחיה = ש׳ : May he live
לאורך = ל׳ : for many
ימים = י׳ : years
טובים = ט׳ : in comfort
אמן = א׳ : Amen.

Shema: lit., hear; see *Kiriyath Shema*.

Shemone Esre: lit., eighteen; also, the Eighteen Benedictions recited silently three times a day; instituted by the Men of the Great Assembly.

Shemoth: lit., Names (referring to the twelve sons of Israel); the Book of Exodus.

shemayim: heaven.

shem u'malchuth: lit., the Name (of G-d) and kingship; referring to the two major components of a beracha. See Berachoth 40b, *Orech Chaim* 214.

shin (ש): the 21st letter of the Hebrew alphabet; has numerical value of 300.

Shir HaShirim: Song of Songs, included in the *Tenach* and written by King Solomon; "While all the Writing are holy, *Shir HaShirim* is the holy of holies" (*Mishna Yadayim* 3:5).

sh'lemah: complete, whole.

sh'patorani: "who has freed me"; this blessing, as well as the source for making a *seudath* Bar Mitzvah, are found in the *Shulchan Aruch, Orech Chaim* 225:2, Rama.

shtibel'ach: (Yiddish) small rooms; a small Chassidic Beit Midrash; today in Israel it also refers to a building containing a number of small shuls.

shuk: market place.

shul: (Yiddish) synagogue.

Shulchan Aruch: "The Prepared Table"; complete codification of Jewish law by Rabbi Yosef Karo of Safet, Israel (1488-1575); divided into four parts: (1) *Orech Chaim* (Way of Life) concerning the daily, weekly, monthly, yearly cycle of mitzvoth (e.g., tefillin, blessings, Shabbat); (2) *Yoreh De'ah* (Going Forth of Knowledge) concerning dietary laws, woman's purity, vows, learning Torah, circumcision, honoring parents, charity, mezuza, mourning; (3) *Choshen Mishpat* (Breastplate of Judgement) concerning judges, testimony, and civil cases; (4) *Even HaEzer* (The Helping Stone) concerning marriage and divorce.

siddur (-im): prayer book; lit., order; although the order of prayers dates back to the Men of the Great Assembly, the earliest prayer books are those of Rabbi Amram Gaon and Rabbi Saadia Gaon (c. 900), followed by the *Machzor Vitri* (c. 1100). Cf., *minhag*.

simcha (-oth): festive occasion.

Simchat Beit HaShoevah: The rejoicing that took place on the Temple Mount every night during the Festival of Booths. After watching the *tzaddikim* dance all night long, everyone marched down to the nearby water-spring of Shiloach in order to fill a pitcher with its water. This water was poured on the altar during the morning service in the Temple. See *Succah* 51a-53b. "One who has not seen the *Simchat Beit HaShoevah* has never witnessed a complete event of rejoicing" (*Mishna Succah* 5:2).

simon tov: good sign, auspicious; name of popular Jewish religious song.

siyaita d'shemaya: (Aramaic) with Heaven's help.

sofer: scribe; one who is competent at writing mezuzoth, tefillin, and *Sifre Torah*.

S'TaM (סת"ם): abbreviation for **S**efer Torah, **T**efillin, **M**ezuza. These three must be written on parchment with a quill and special ink.

succah: lit., booth; "You shall dwell in booths seven days... that your generations may know that I made the children of Israel to dwell in booths when I brought them out of the land of Egypt" (Lev. 23:43).

T

tallit: prayer shawl; lit., a cover; always made of four corners with fringes attached to each corner. Cf., *tzitzits*.

Talmid (-ei) Chacham (-im): Torah scholar; "A *Talmid Chacham* who does not have his inside like his outside (whose *midoth* are not on the same high level as his Torah knowledge) is not a *Talmid Chacham*" (*Yoma* 82b).

Talmud Torah: the place where one studies Torah; religious school for youngsters until the age of Bar Mitzvah; also, learning Torah.

Talmudic: from the Talmud (*Gemora*); referring to the Babylonian and Jerusalem discussions on the *Mishna*.

Tannaim (sing. *Tanna*): teacher; the Torah sages mentioned in the *Mishna* and *Braiytah* who lived during the period of the Second Temple and afterwards until the death of Rabbi Yehuda HaNassi in 218 C.E.

Targum: the Aramaic translation of Scripture; Onkelos the proselyte wrote down the *Targum* of *Chumash* which had orally been transmitted to him. Yonatan ben Uziel did the same with the books of the Prophets (See *Megilla* 3a).

Taryag (תרי״ג): Abbreviation for 613, as follows:

ת׳	:	400
ר׳	:	200
י׳	:	10
ג׳	:	3
תרי״ג		613

Cf., *mitzvah.*

tefillah (*-oth*): prayer, supplication; "There are two prerequisites for prayer to be acceptable: (1) that one's prayer should not be a burden; (2) that the prayer itself should be pure" (G'ra, *Even Sh'lemah*).

tefillin: phylactery; The hand-tefillin and the head-tefillin each are one of the 613 commandments; one who wears tefillin will live a longer life, as the verse in Isaiah 38:16 says, "O L-rd, with these things men live" (*Menachoth* 44a-b).

Tehillim: Book of Psalms, composed by King David (906-836 B.C.E.), including some psalms by the Ten Elders (Adam, Abraham, Moses, etc.; see *Baba Batra* 14b); "Corresponding to the Five Books of the Torah which Moses gave to Israel, King David gave the Psalms which he divided into five books" (*Midrash*).

Tenach (תנ״ך): Scripture, the Written Law, consisting of twenty-four books; lit., the abbreviation of:

תורה = ת׳ : Torah (Five Books of Moses)
נביאים = נ׳ : Prophets
כתובים = כ׳ : Writings

teshuva: repentance; lit., to return; "Return, unruly children, and I will heal your backslidings" (Jeremiah 3:22). See *Yoma* 86a. Cf., *baalei teshuva.*

tikun chatzoth: prayers of mourning recited over the destruction of our Temple and the exile of the *Shechina*; said after midnight (*chatzoth*) except during the three weeks prior to *Tisha B'av* when they may be recited also in the afternoon; not said on Shabbat and Yom Tov. See *Orech Chaim* 1:1.

titura: lit., bridge, the base of the tefillin.

Torah: the Law; from the root to show the way; generally referring to (1) Scripture, the Written Law (*Torah she-bichtav*); or (2) both the Written and the Oral Law (*Torah she-baal-peh*), i.e., the 613 mitzvoth along with their explanations and interpretations. "Where there is no flour (i.e., food), there is no Torah; where there is no Torah, there is no flour (what is life for without Torah?)" (*Pirke Avoth* 3:21).

Tosefoth: The Torah sages of France and Germany, the disciples of Rashi (c. 1105-1300), who closely examined and discussed Rashi's commentary on the Talmud, as well as the *Gemora* itself.

totofath (-oth): frontlets, referring to the head tefillin; a Mishnaic word meaning headband (*Shabbat* 6:1).

t'refeh: lit., torn apart; an animal rendered unfit because one of the internal organs is damaged or diseased. Cf., *n'velah*.

tzaddik (*-im*): righteous person; "The *tzaddik* eats to satisfy his soul" (Proverbs 13:25); "The *tzaddikim*, even when they are dead, are called living" (*Berachoth* 18a). Cf., *Talmid Chacham*.

tzedaka: charity; "A person shall never become poor by giving charity, nor shall anything bad happen to him because he gave it, as it says, 'The work of righteousness (*tzedaka*) shall be peace' (Isaiah 32:17)" (Rambam). Cf., *Yoreh De'ah* 247-259.

tzitzits: fringes; "You shall make fringes upon the four corners of your coverings, with which you cover yourself" (Deut. 22:12). The *tzitzits* reminds us of the *Taryag mitzvoth* : the numerical value of the word ציצית is 600, and with the eight threads and the five knots, total 613 (Rashi, Numbers 15:39).

Y

ya'amod: will he stand up, arise.

Yehoshuah: Joshua.

yeshiva: place of learning Torah; academy of Jewish studies; lit., sitting; the main emphasis in learning is the Oral Law, the *Mishna* and *Gemora*.

yeshiva ketannah: the place of learning Torah for young men from the age of Bar Mitzvah until the age of eighteen. Cf., *Talmud Torah*.

yetzer-harah: the evil inclination; "The Holy One blessed be He said to the Jewish People: 'My children, I created the *yetzer-harah* and I have created the Torah as its antidote' " (*Kiddushin* 30b).

yetzer-tov: good inclination; "Better is a poor and wise child (this is the *yetzer-tov* — Rashi), than an old and foolish king (—the *yetzer-harah*)" (Eccl. 4:13).

Yid: (Yiddish) a Jew.

Yirmiyahu: Jeremiah the Prophet, who prophesied at the time of the destruction of the First Temple; also wrote the Book of Lamentations.

Yom Tov: festive day; in *halacha*, a day prescribed by the Torah as a holiday (1st and 7th days of Passover, *Shavuoth, Rosh Hashannah, Yom Kippur, Sukkoth, Shemini Atzeret*), having all the restrictions of Shabbat, except that cooking, transferring fire and carrying in a public domain are all permitted.

Yona: Jonah.

yud (י): the tenth letter of the Hebrew alphabet.

Z

Zeide: (Yiddish) grandfather.

Zohar: Book of Splendor; the Kabbalistic teachings of Rabbi Shimon bar Yochai, written down by his disciple Rabbi Abba about 120 years after the destruction of the Second Temple.

z'tl (זצ"ל): abbreviation for:

ז' = זכר : May the memory
צ' = צדיק : of the righteous
ל' = לברכה : be for a blessing.

Added after mentioning the name of someone who passed away; based on the verse in Prov. 10:7.

Biographical Sketches

AGASSI, Rabbi Shimon S. (1852 — 8 Av 1914).

A great Sephardi *dayan* and kabbalist from Baghdad. At the age of thirteen, when the custom was that a young man apprentice himself in a trade or profession, he wholeheartedly chose to study Torah. His diligence at his studies was phenomenal, and he quickly mastered all areas of Torah knowledge. He became the leader of Baghdad Jewry after the death of the Ben Ish Chai in 1909.

Among his written works are *Imre Shimon* (on Mussar), *Bnei Aaron* (on Kabbala) and *Foundations of the Torah*.

BENYAMIN ZEV: See Maggid of Zalotshov.

CHASAM SOFER: Rabbi Moshe Sofer (7 Tishre 1763 — 25 Tishre 1840).

One of the great *gedolim* of the past 200 years, he was a child prodigy whose genius was recognized by the leaders of the generation. By the age of seven, he had memorized several tractates of *Gemora*. He entered the yeshiva of Rabbi Natan Adler at the age of nine and followed his rebbe until his rebbe's death in 1800, calling him the "crown of my head." At 18 he began teaching Torah publicly.

In 1808, he settled in Pressburg, and opened a yeshiva which became the most important in Western Europe. Hundreds flocked there to learn Torah, and with each *talmid* he had a personal relationship.

His second wife, the daughter of Rabbi Akiva Eiger, bore him all his ten children.

He is known after the title of his responsas, *Chasam Sofer* (on the *Shulchan Aruch*). We also have by him *Chidushei Chasam Sofer* (on the Talmud) and *Torath Moshe* (on the Torah).

CHAZON ISH: Rabbi Avraham Yeshaya Karelitz (11 Cheshvan 1879 — 15 Cheshvan 1954): *Gadol HaDor*.

Born in Kosova before World War I, he moved to Vilna where his greatness became known, especially to the Rabbi of Vilna, Chaim Ozer Grodzensky. The latter often took counsel with the young Torah scholar before making important halachic decisions.

After 15 years in Vilna, he decided to move to Israel. By then his first halachic work, *Chazon Ish* ("Vision of a Man"), had revealed to the Torah world the greatness and clarity of his mind. In 1933, he settled in Bnei Brak and made his home a living thoroughfare of Torah and *chesed*. Thousands came to him with personal problems, health matters and Torah issues. All left with clear answers that helped guide them in life. Although childless, he became the father of a whole generation.

He stressed the study of Torah as the key to success in life, and writes, "The idea of *hathmadah* (diligent perserverance) in Torah study is not judged by the amount of time given, but by the devotion of one's whole being to the one aim of studying Torah. One hour of intense study and seriousness is worth more than many idle ones...In order to reach *hathmadah* one must wage a war between the mind and desirous elements within oneself."

His classic halachic work, the *Chazon Ish*, covered the whole *Shulchan Aruch* and, over the years, was published in 23 volumes.

CHOFETZ CHAIM: Rabbi Yisroel Meir Kagan (11 Shevat 1839 — 24 Elul 1933): *Gadol HaDor*.

After learning in Vilna and following his marriage, he settled in Radan, Poland. There, he learned Torah day and night, often sleeping on a bench in the Beit Midrash rather than going home to bed.

At the age of thirty, he published an in-depth book on the laws of *lashon hara* called the *Chofetz Chaim* (Lover of Life) which was acclaimed as a masterpiece. In 1875 he wrote a sequel called *Shemirath HaLashon*. In the same year, he began work on a monumental project which would consume twenty years his life. This work was the *Mishna Berura*, a halachic commentary on the *Shulchan Aruch, Orech Chaim*, in which he discussed every *halacha*, both its source and its contemporary application. The success of the *Mishna Berura* in our time is uncomparable as almost everyone studies it and many *shiurim* are given in it.

The Chofetz Chaim's warmth and love of his fellow Jew was phenomenal. Once someone found him reciting *Tehillim* with great emotion. When asked if someone in his family was seriously ill, he answered, "A woman I never met before came to me today and asked me to pray for her son who is very sick."

ELIMELECH: Rebbe of Lizensk (died: 21 Adar 1787). Chassidic Rebbe. As the chief disciple of the Maggid of Mezeritch, he gained great insights into *avodath HaShem*, which later served as a basis of his teachings. After spending eight years in self-exile, he settled down and soon attracted a large following. He was among the first *Admors* (*rebbes*) in the Chassidic family tree.

His commentary to the *Chumash, Noam Elimelech*, was published posthumously by his son and is considered one of the classics of Chassidic literature. The *Sanz* Rebbe (*Divre Chaim*) once commented that if he were to write a *perush* to *Noam Elimelech*, it would be as long as the *perush* which the *Beit Yosef* wrote on the *Tur*.

Rebbe Elimelech also wrote the famous *Tzetel Katon* ("A Short Message") on *avodath HaShem* which is often quoted at the back of many *seforim*. He wrote: "Learning *Gemora* and *Tosefoth*, as well as the *aggadoth*, are one of the keys to purifying the soul."

Among his many great disciples were the Rebbe of Lublin, the Maggid of Koznitz, the author of *Me'or V'Shemesh*, and Rebbe Moshe Leib of Sassov.

EMDEN, Rabbi Yaakov of (1698 — 30 Nisan 1776).
The son of the *Chacham Tzvi*, of Altona, Germany, Rabbi Emden received his early Torah education directly from his father. At 17 he left for Brody and later, after his marriage, moved to Amsterdam. At 30 he became the Chief Rabbi of Emden, but resigned after four years, choosing instead a career as a Torah writer and publisher in his native Altona. He printed his own *seforim* and gave them away free of charge to whoever wanted them. For a livelihood, he was a jewel merchant.

He grieved over the unexpected death of his wife and son until he became seriously ill. Later, after he recovered, he remarried and had three sons.

He was universally recognized as a Torah giant and contributed many important works including a commentary on the *siddur (Beit Yaakov)*, *Lechem Shamayim* (on *Mishna*), *Migdal Oz* (on *mussar*) and glosses to all of *Shas*.

He was also known as the *Yavetz*, which is an abbreviation of ***YA***akov ***Be***n ***Tz***vi.

EVED HAMELECH: See *Houminer, Rabbi Shmuel*.

HIRSCH, *Rabbi Samson Raphael* (24 Sivan 1808 — 27 Teveth 1888).

Born in Hamburg, Germany, he diligently studied Torah and was awarded *s'micha* (to be a rabbi) at the age of 20, and later received a doctorate from the University of Bonn.

At 23 he became Chief Rabbi of Oldenburg and there he wrote *Horeb*, his masterpiece on the meaning of the mitzvoth. To test the market, his publisher asked first to print a shorter book. This was the famous *Nineteen Letters* (1836).

A vibrantly strong opponent of the secularism which was sweeping through Germany, he emphasized the importance of Jewish education and, through his leadership, transformed Frankfort-on-Main into a Torah stronghold.

His greatness as an important contributor to Torah literature was recognized with his phenomenal commentary on the *Chumash* (1867-78) and on the Book of Psalms.

HOUMINER, *Rabbi Shmuel* (25 Tishre 1914 — 19 Sivan 1977).

He was born in Jerusalem and studied at the renowned Etz Chaim Yeshiva under the guidance of the Rosh Yeshiva, Rabbi Meltzer.

At the age of twenty-six he published his first work, *Ikray Dinim*, a concise version of the Chofetz Chaim's laws on *lashon harah*.

Rabbi Houminer was universally known for his profound humility and deep love of his fellow man. He refused all titles and formal positions and remained throughout his life a quiet, very personable *tzaddik*. Many came to his house for advice or to discuss a wide range of Torah topics; to each and every one he extended his whole being.

His masterpiece, *Eved HaMelech* (Servant of the King), is a comprehensive compilation of mitzvoth and practices derived from *Tenach* published in ten volumes. Among his other works are *Sefer Kedusha, Mitzvat HaBetachon* (on trust in G-d), and *Olath Tamid* (a commentary on the siddur).

MAGGID OF ZALOTSHOV: *Rebbe Yechiel Michel* (1726 — 25 Elul 1786). When Rebbe Yechiel was a child, his father used to take him to visit the Baal Shem Tov. When he grew up, he became one of the leading disciples of the Maggid of Mezeritch, the main *talmid* of the B'esht.

He lived in great poverty most of his life and maintained his family as a *melamed* (school teacher). His gifts as a seer and orator aroused thousands of people to repentance.

In 1759, he left his home in Brody, Poland, because of the great *misnagged* sentiments there and moved to Zalotshov where he became known as the Maggid of Zalotshov.

He left five sons, all *gedolim* in their own right. His youngest son, Benyamin Zev, continued in his father's footsteps to be a light to thousands and spread the teachings of Chassidus until his death on 3 Nisan 1822.

MAHARSHA: *Rabbi Shmuel Eliezer Eidels* (1555 — 5 Kislev 1632). Born in Cracow, Poland, he traced his lineage to Rabbi Yehuda HaChassid (*Sefer Chassidim*), and he was related to the Maharal of Prague.

He headed various yeshivoth in different communities — Posen, Kelm, Lublin, Ostrog — and was able to maintain them through the wealth of his virtuous wife Edel. In recognition of her benevolence he added the surname Eidels to his name.

He was the *gadol hador* and unique in his direct approach at studying *Gemora*. His *Chidushei Halachoth* (1617) and *Chidushei Aggadoth* (1627) are printed at the back of every *Gemora* and are invaluable for understanding the basic talmudic train of reasoning. The Chazon Ish stressed the importance of learning the Maharsha.

His house was always open to the wayfarer and the poor, providing them with food and lodging.

Maharsha is an abbreviation of **MO**reinu **HAR**av **SH**muel **E**idels.

NA'EH, Rabbi Avraham Chaim (died: 20 Tamuz 1954).

A renowned scholar, Rabbi Na'eh was a leading *posek* (authority in *halacha*). He wrote *Piskei HaSiddur, Shiurei Torah* and *Ketzoth HaShulchan*.

NOAM ELIMELECH: See *Elimelech, Rebbe of Lizensk.*

RABBENU TAM: *Rabbi Yaakov ben Meir* (c. 1100 — 1170).

Rashi's grandson, Rabbenu Tam was one of the greatest *Baalei Tosefoth*. His older brother, the Rashbam, was one of his teachers. Because of his tremendous clarity of thought and ability to express clearly his ideas, he became known as Rabbenu Tam (Clear One) and was one of the leading sages of his time.

Once, after a long, involved debate with Rabbi Ephraim, one of the *Baalei Tosefoth*, over the question of whether the tefillin strap has to be reknotted every day or not, Rabbenu Tam stood up and exclaimed, "Moshe Rabbenu, come down! Moshe Rabbenu, come down!" When Moshe Rabbenu came down into the yeshiva, Rabbenu Tam said to him, "I hold that we don't have to reknot the tefillin straps every day, and that you never commanded this in the Torah that you received from HaShem." Moshe nodded in agreement and immediately left.

He wrote *Sefer HaYashar*.

RAMBAM: *Rabbi Moshe ben Maimon* (14 Nisan 1133 — 20 Teveth 1205).

Born in Cordova, Spain, the Rambam failed to apply himself to his studies in his early years, causing his father to whip him and finally expel him from the house. That night, he slept in a *Beit Kenesset* and awoke feeling a new willpower to devote himself to Torah. After learning in another city where his genius matured, he returned to Cordova and spoke before the congregation on Shabbat. His father was amazed to hear his son speak so deeply on a Torah subject and, afterwards, reunited with him and blessed him.

Around 1165, he left Spain, and after half a year in *Eretz Yisroel*, he settled in Egypt. There, his fame and reputation spread far and wide. His *perush* to *Mishnayoth*, begun in Spain, was completed seven years later in Egypt. The Sultan of Egypt took him as his private physician and attested to the Rambam's supremacy over his own counselors in the seven known wisdoms of the world.

He spent ten years (1170-80) writing the *Yad Chazakah (Mishna Torah)* where he clearly systematized all Torah knowledge and drew out the conclusions of the *Gemora* on what the law should be in every case. This work was a monumental turning point in the development of the Oral Law. The immense success and acceptance of this fundamental work can be grasped by the number of commentaries that have been written on it.

On the night that he finished it, the Rambam dreamt that his father together with another man came to visit him. His father introduced the stranger, "This is Moshe Rabbenu!" The Rambam was stunned. His father continued, "I have come to see what you have accomplished." When the Rambam showed him the manuscript, his father commented, "Yeshar Ko'ach (May you have even greater strength)!!!"

The Rambam also wrote *Sefer HaMitzvoth* and the *Guide to the Perplexed* (both originally in Arabic).

RASHI: *Rabbenu Shlomo Yitzchaki* (1040 — 1105).

Yitzchaki was not Rashi's last name; it was given in honor of his father, Rabbi Yitzchak, himself a great scholar.

From his youth, his Torah learning was spectacular. Over the years, he collected everything that he had learned from his rabbis, as well as his own interpretations, and wrote them down in notebooks (*kuntrasim*). These *kuntrasim* were later used by his disciples — *Tosefoth* — who called Rashi by the title *Perush HaKuntras*.

At the age of 33, he left his native France and went into self-exile for seven years, having already completed his commentary to the *Chumash* and most of the Talmud. One reason for his wandering throughout Europe and the Middle East was to see if anyone else had already written a commentary. Upon his return, seeing that there was a need for his work, he published his *perush*. Over the years, he rewrote it three times, with the text in our *Gemora* being his final revision.

He had three daughters but no sons. Rabbenu Tam and the Rashbam were among his grandsons. Rabbenu Tam said: "Although I could write an equally good *perush* to *Shas* as Rashi, his *perush* to the

Chumash is unmatchable." Indeed, everyone agrees that Rashi's commentaries to *Shas* and *Tenach* are absolutely essential for understanding the text.

The *Chida* comments: "Rashi was extremely precise in the wording of his commentary: he would hint to ideas by the change of a single letter." Rashi's greatness is proven by the thousands upon thousands who carefully study daily his every word.

SERAF (HAKODESH): *Rebbe Uri of Starilisk* (died 23 Elul 1826).
He studied under the Admor of Karlin, Rebbe Shlomo, and was praised for knowing the Rambam by heart.

Even before his conception, the Maggid of Mezeritch foretold to his mother that she would bear a son who would cast a great light in the world.

The vibrant intensity of his *tefilloth* succeeded in bringing many people closer in *avodath HaShem*, as well as earning him the title *Seraf HaKodesh*, meaning tremendous enthusiasm and cleaving through prayer.

For the layman, he stressed the importance of learning *niglah* (the revealed Torah) and restraining oneself from studying *nistar* (the secrets of Torah).

URI, *Rebbe of Starilisk*: See previous entry.

YEYBI SABA: *Rabbi Yaakov Yosef* (1749 — 20 Tishre 1801).
The only son of the Maggid of Ostraha, Yeybi Saba learned Torah from both his father and the Maggid of Mezeritch. After his father passed away in 1766, he replaced him as maggid and remained in that position for 36 years until his death in 1801.

He was known as a wonder worker and a deep Torah scholar. His short pamphlet, *Morah Mikdosh*, on the holiness of the synagogue, was first published in 1781, and copies were hung in many shuls throughout Europe. He also wrote *Rav Yeybi* on the Torah, *Tehillim*, and *chidushim* on *Shas*.

Yeybi is an abbreviation of **Y**a**a**kov **Y**osef **b**en **Y**ehuda.

I would like to express my gratitude to KOLEL AMERICA "TIFERETH JERUSALEM" (12 Chesed L'Abraham St, Jerusalem), THE RABBI MEYER BAAL HANESS CHARITY, for lending a helpful hand in the publication of this book.

Their prolific activities in spreading Torah are well known. They help support thousands of Americans and Canadians who study in over 150 yeshivoth and Colels throughout our Holy Land. Included among these recipients are *talmidei chachamim*, widows and orphans, *baalei teshuva* and proselytes. They have a well organized system of financial-aid programs for the festivals, for couples who are preparing for their marriage, for a newborn member of a family, for purchasing a flat, for those who are ill, as well as a free loan office (on a long-term repayment system) and many other activities.

May they be blessed with all the *berachoth* that are given to those who truly dedicate themselves to the needs of the Torah public. May the Almighty repay them and increase and magnify their efforts.

ואלו יעמדו על הברכה

הנדיב ר׳ חיים דוד כהן הי״ו לעלוי נשמת
הרה״ח אריה בן הר״ר אהרן וגנאר זצ״ל
נפטר ה׳ תמוז תשל״ט

שמואל מליץ ז״ל
נלב״ע י׳ טבת תשמ״ג

ת.נ.צ.ב.ה.

הנדיב ר׳ שלום שורץ הי״ו
זכרון עולם
לעלוי נשמת
אמו בילא בת משה ע״ה
נפטרה ט׳ ניסן תשמ״ג

ת.נ.צ.ב.ה.